P9-DXT-874

5/19

UP FOR AIR

LAURIE MORRISON

AMULET BOOKS • NEW YORK

Cataloging-in-Publication Data has been applied for and may be obtained from the Library of Congress.

ISBN 978-1-4197-3366-6

Text copyright © 2019 Laurie Morrison
Book design by Hana Anouk Nakamura

Published in 2019 by Amulet Books, an imprint of ABRAMS. All rights reserved. No portion of this book may be reproduced, stored in a retrieval system, or transmitted in any form or by any means, mechanical, electronic, photocopying, recording, or otherwise, without written permission from the publisher.

Printed and bound in U.S.A.
10 9 8 7 6 5 4 3 2 1

Amulet Books are available at special discounts when purchased in quantity for premiums and promotions as well as fundraising or educational use. Special editions can also be created to specification. For details, contact specialsales@abramsbooks.com or the address below.

Amulet Books® is a registered trademark of Harry N. Abrams, Inc.

ABRAMS The Art of Books
195 Broadway, New York, NY 10007
abramsbooks.com

For my mom, Elizabeth Morrison, with so much love and gratitude

Chapter 1

The loudest kind of quiet filled the classroom. Pens scratched paper, erasers squeaked, and desk legs groaned as the clock on the wall *tick-tick-tick*ed. Faster and faster, it seemed, even though Annabelle knew that was impossible.

She was almost out of time.

And the thing was, she got *extra* time. She and the four other seventh graders with "learning accommodations" got forty-five minutes longer than the rest of the kids, who'd already pushed in their chairs and turned in their exam booklets and burst into the hallways to celebrate the start of summer. But forty-five extra minutes didn't do Annabelle any good when her brain had gone as hazy as the harbor on a foggy day.

She ran her fingertip across the skinny blue lines in the booklet where she was supposed to be writing her essay. The essay that counted for 25 percent of the history exam grade, as Mr. Derrickson had told them over and over. She traced one, two, three lines across the page and wished she were staring down at the thick black lines along the bottom of the pool.

She didn't need those black lines to guide her from one end of the pool to the other anymore. Her body always stayed straight, and she knew exactly how many strokes to take before it was time to flip underwater and push off the wall, propelling herself back the other way. But she still liked knowing they were there, as familiar as everything else about swimming. The glint of sunlight on the pool's pale blue surface. The mingled scents of sunscreen, chlorine, and greasy snack bar food. The splash of diving in and the cool welcome of the water.

The learning specialist, Ms. Ames, put her hand on Annabelle's wrist.

"Just write down anything you remember, okay?" she whispered. "Like we talked about. That way Mr. Derrickson can give you credit for what you know."

So Annabelle took three deep breaths, the way she always did before a race, and tried to tune out the clock's echoing tick and the other kids' frantic writing.

She managed to fill up half the page . . . but she knew exactly what Mr. Derrickson would do when he read what she'd written. He'd scrawl question marks in the margins with his green pen. He'd write, "Irrelevant," and "Please answer the question," and "Where is your thesis?"

She flipped through the rest of the test. All those multiple-choice questions with all those choices that sounded right. The fill-in-the-blank section Mr. Derrickson had insisted was "easy-peasy." "Automatic points for anybody who's studied at all." Right.

"Okay," Ms. Ames said from the front of the room. "Put your pens and pencils down, please. And congratulations! You're officially done with seventh grade!"

Two kids whooped and high-fived each other. Annabelle looked at the essay she'd barely started, barely holding back tears as she gathered up her things.

She managed to echo Ms. Ames's "Have a good summer" before stumbling into the hallways that had emptied out almost an hour ago. When Mia and Jeremy and everyone else had all gone to lunch without her.

The other four extra-time kids were all boarding students, so they told Annabelle they'd see her at middle school closing ceremonies and headed to the cafeteria or the dorms. Annabelle pushed open the side door, stepping into the bright June sunshine.

She gulped in the island air—a little bit salty if you really paid attention, even this far from the ocean. It was over, anyway. Seventh grade was finally done, and summer stretched out ahead of her, full of adventures with Mia and Jeremy and summer swim team practices at the pool, where most of the kids didn't go to the Academy and she got to be Annabelle the star butterflyer, not Annabelle who could never finish her work on time at school.

Mom's car was waiting at the curb, and she rolled down the window. "Belle! How'd it go, honey? Did we study the right things? Did you feel ready?"

"I'm never ready for Mr. Derrickson's tests."

Annabelle plopped down onto the hot front seat, tossed her things on the floor, and slammed the door closed.

Mom's eyebrows folded in, forming that tiny worry line right in the middle. That was how she used to look at Dad, back when things got really bad. And it was how she looked at Annabelle now, way, way too often.

"Well, you worked so hard," Mom said. "I'm sure all that effort paid off."

Then she nodded. As if she could nod those words into being true. She patted Annabelle's knee and reached up to grip the steering wheel, her silver bracelets clinking. Mitch had given her one of those bracelets for each of their wedding anniversaries. She had three so far, and she wore them all the time.

"Where to?" she asked as she pulled away from the curb. "My next meeting isn't until two. We could go out for a special lunch. Do you want to call Mitch to see if he's free? I know he'll want to celebrate with you, too."

Annabelle watched out the window as they drove along the school's winding driveway, past dorms and fields and high school kids who sat on the grass, laughing as they signed each other's yearbooks. Past the gray-shingled office where they'd come for her admissions interview two years ago—the summer before sixth grade, when she and Mom and Mitch had first moved to Gray Island.

The Academy was a boarding school, mostly, for sixth-to-twelfth-grade students from the mainland. But Mom had read on their website that they "strive to be a community school" and set aside financial aid for "qualified day students" who live on the island. So she'd filled out an application for Annabelle, and somehow Annabelle had gotten in.

Because barely any other island kids had applied, probably. Because most island kids thought everybody at the Academy was snobby.

"You must be hungry, huh?" Mom said.

She was, but if they went out to lunch in town, Mom and Mitch would know everybody and everybody would ask about school because that's what everybody *always* asked about. And anyway, after this morning, her whole body ached with the need to swim.

"Actually can you drop me off at the pool?" she asked. "I can eat there."

"But you don't have practice today," Mom pointed out.

"Yeah, but we did yesterday," Annabelle reminded her, as if she needed to be reminded. "And I really need to swim today, since I skipped it."

Mom had made Annabelle stay home from summer team practice to squeeze in a few more hours of studying, not that those extra hours had done any good.

Mom sighed, and Annabelle sort of wished Mitch had been the one to pick her up. Mitch would have agreed to take her to the pool in an instant because he *got* it—how important it was for Annabelle to train. How good she was, and how great she could be.

"You probably have lots of work anyway, right?" Annabelle said. "With all the summer people wanting you to plan all their parties? Could we do takeout from Lombardi's tonight instead? I'm in a gnocchi mood."

Mom hesitated at the stop sign, but she turned left instead of right, toward the pool instead of back to town. Annabelle's shoulders relaxed for the first time since she'd sat down to start her test that morning.

"All right, Belle. You deserve to celebrate how you want. The pool and Lombardi's it is."

Mom probably wouldn't feel that way if she'd seen how little Annabelle had written for her essay, but Annabelle kept her mouth shut and watched all the giant vacation homes they passed, mostly occupied again now that summer was finally starting.

When they got to the pool, Mom said the same exact things she always did: to be safe and reapply sunscreen and drink plenty of water. Then she leaned over to give Annabelle an extra-tight, extra-long hug.

"I'll come back to get you after my two o'clock meeting," she said into Annabelle's ear. "And, hey. I'm proud of you no matter what. You know that, right?"

Annabelle nodded as she pulled away from Mom's hug and then stepped out of the car. But did that even count, the kind of pride you didn't have to do anything good to earn?

Chapter 2

After Annabelle ate lunch at the snack bar, she changed into her new black racing suit and lowered herself into an open lap lane between two grown-ups. One of them was swimming a smooth, quick freestyle, and the other bobbed up and down in a slow breaststroke.

She pushed off the wall and started to swim, feeling the familiar pinch of her goggles and watching bubbles stream ahead of her as she blew out air.

Stroke. Stroke. Stroke. Stroke.

Once she reached the other end, she flip-turned and pushed off, her strong quad muscles launching her forward. Her mind cleared, just like always, and her arms and legs took over. Each time she came up for a breath, she heard a burst of noise—people chatting, little kids shouting by the baby pool—but then her head was back under where she couldn't hear anything other than the swish, pull, and kick of her own body. By the time she reached the wall again, her muscles itched to speed up, and it felt so good to pick up her pace.

This wasn't like school, where she was always aware of what everybody else was doing: who finished tests early, who wrote so much that they had to ask for extra paper, who hissed a "Yes!" when a teacher handed back an assignment. In the pool, she could sense where other swimmers were without wasting any focus on them. She was only vaguely aware that the distance between her and the freestyler in the next lane stretched longer and longer as she swam faster and faster. She barely even noticed when the two other lap swimmers finished and got out.

After her fingertips touched the wall at the end of her last lap, she was surprised to see an older girl standing over her, clapping.

She pushed her goggles up her forehead. It was Elisa Price, dressed for the fourteen-and-up team's practice in a navy and yellow team suit. Annabelle was used to seeing Elisa with a swim cap on, so it took a second to recognize her with her thick brown curls loose around her freckled face.

"Well if it isn't the girl who broke all my under-fourteen fly records!" Elisa said, and Annabelle grinned.

"I still have to shave off some time to beat your freestyle ones, though," she replied as she pushed herself out of the water.

Elisa laughed, showing the little gap between her front teeth that made her look friendly and unintimidating, even though she was so tall and strong and finishing her sophomore year at Gray Island High.

"Yeah, I don't think that's gonna be a problem, judging by what I just saw," she said.

Other high school swimmers were here, too, which meant it was later than Annabelle had realized. Her friend Jeremy's older sister, Kayla, waved from across the pool, and two guys—Connor Madison and Jordan Bernstein—were over by the lifeguard stand, yanking off their T-shirts and pulling on swim caps as they laughed with the new lifeguard.

Thick clouds had covered up the sun, so Annabelle wrapped her arms around herself to stop shivering.

"Go dry off," Elisa said. "But good to see you, Annabelle. And I'll try to emotionally prepare myself for seeing my name erased from the rest of the under-fourteen record boards this summer."

She swiped at her eyes as if she were tearing up and then gave Annabelle's shoulder a squeeze.

Annabelle passed Connor and Jordan on the way to get her towel, and when she walked by, she heard Connor's low voice.

"Wow. Looks like Hummingbird's all grown up," he said. Quietly, but not *that* quietly.

And when she glanced up, his green eyes were on her, laser focused. As if she were more interesting than any of the high school girls who were always giggling at his jokes and finding reasons to touch his arm.

As if he definitely didn't see her the way everybody used to—as the little girl who was fast enough to swim with the bigger kids but had to move her arms and legs hummingbird-quick to keep up.

As she wrapped herself in her towel, her belly went as warm as if she'd chugged hot chocolate. Her new black suit fit differently than her other racing suits did. The straps were thin and the front dipped low enough that she could see the freckle in the middle of her chest— the one most of her shirts covered up. Her other racing suits flattened her out, but this one didn't. And the leg openings were cut extra high, which meant her legs looked extra long.

Connor Madison had noticed.

Connor Madison, who was finishing his freshman year at the high school and was so funny and charming that even the seniors flirted with him. She couldn't wait to tell Mia. The other day, she and Mia had agreed that Connor was the cutest boy at the pool.

Right now, Annabelle didn't feel at all like the girl who had barely written anything on her history exam essay.

She felt powerful. Unstoppable. *Extraordinary.*

Chapter 3

By the next week, Annabelle had convinced herself her grades wouldn't be *that* terrible.

After all, she *had* worked really, really hard. She'd gone to every extra help session. She'd reviewed with her tutor every day during lunch and with Mom every night at home. She'd definitely failed Mr. Derrickson's final, but exams didn't count for *that* much of the overall grades. And anyway she'd turned in all that extra credit.

On the morning that grades were scheduled to be posted online, Mom sat next to her at the kitchen table as she opened up her laptop and logged into her school account.

Her hand shook as she tried to click on the link that read, "Annabelle Marie Wilner. Seventh Grade Report Card."

"You okay?" Mom asked, and Annabelle knew without looking that the worry line had formed between her eyebrows again. "I can leave the room. Do you want to check by yourself?"

Annabelle shook her head. The grades would be mailed home, too. It's not like she could keep them a secret. She took three deep breaths and clicked.

And then she jerked her hand back as if the trackpad had burned her finger.

B+ in science. B– in math. C in Spanish. C in English. C– in history.

Mom gasped when she saw the grades, then covered her mouth as if she could force the gasp back in.

Three Cs. After all that work.

Three Cs on her final seventh-grade report card was the absolute best she could do.

"Oh, Belle." Mom reached out for a hug, but Annabelle ducked away and stood.

"I'm . . . I'm meeting Jeremy and Mia. I have to go."

Mom's worry line was etched in so deep that Annabelle thought it might get stuck there, the way kids used to say your eyes could get stuck if you crossed them for too long.

"You did your best, honey," Mom said. "That's what matters."

Right.

Annabelle hurried to the front hall to grab her things. "I'll be back by three," she called.

"Be safe! Love you!" Mom called back.

Annabelle bolted for the door so Mom wouldn't have to come up with any more lies to make her feel better.

Or to make *herself* feel better. About having a daughter who could only get Cs, no matter how hard she tried.

Outside, the sky was bright and cloudless—the same blue as the hyacinths in bloom all around the island. Annabelle fastened her helmet, dropped her bag in the basket of her bike, and started to ride.

She was meeting Jeremy and Mia at Bluff Point, their favorite summer place. It was right off the bike path, so they were allowed to go by themselves, and far enough away from the fancy neighborhoods full of vacation homes that it was never crowded, even once summer people took over most of the island.

Annabelle usually loved riding her bike. She loved that she made her own breeze, even when the air was hot and still like today. She loved the soft buzz of her tires against the worn pavement and the way she knew just how hard to pedal to get through the patches of sand that sometimes covered the ground. Biking was almost as good as swimming for clearing her head and making her feel completely in control.

But today, she couldn't stop thinking of those Cs on her report card and that look on her mom's face. The shock that Annabelle couldn't do any better. There was something else behind that shock, too. Shame? That Annabelle was her daughter, and she was this bad at school?

And how many more Cs would it take before the school decided that she wasn't a "qualified day student" who deserved special financial aid after all? And what would Mom do then?

Bike tires spun on the ground behind Annabelle, and then there was Jeremy, pulling up beside her. Jeremy would know the right word for that look on Mom's face, if Annabelle told him about it. He knew the right word for everything.

"I saw you from way back by Brambleberry Street, but I didn't think I'd catch you," he said.

"I guess I'm slow today." She forced herself to smile.

Jeremy grinned back. "You? Never."

He'd gotten a haircut since school had ended, so the longish light brown pieces that usually hung out the front and sides of his bike helmet were gone. He wore one of his dad's GREEN CONSTRUCTION T-shirts, and the baggy sleeves hung to his elbows.

"Did you check your grades?" she asked, because it was better to get the topic over with.

"Yeah, I saw them."

And they were probably all As and A-pluses, because that was Jeremy. He had the same kind of "qualified day student" scholarship Annabelle did, but he actually deserved his. He had probably never even considered the possibility of getting a C. He'd be shocked by an A-minus.

"You checked yours, too?" he asked.

"Yep," she replied, then scrambled for something else to talk about. "Hey, any news on Bertha?"

"Yes!"

A man with a little kid on the back of his bike rang his bell to pass. Jeremy fell in behind Annabelle as the man sped by. A summer dad, riding the kind of bike they rented out at the shops in town.

Then Jeremy caught back up, his pale brown eyes wide with excitement. "She pinged near Montauk, and she's heading our way!"

Bertha was a great white shark who'd been spotted off the shore of the island last summer, and Jeremy watched her movements on a shark-tracking app. She was a juvenile—so young that her jaw wasn't strong enough to eat seals or sea lions yet, and she couldn't travel too far from the coast of Long Island, where her home was.

"You think she's going to come back to the island?" Annabelle asked.

In front of them, the summer dad's tires swerved as he hit a patch of sand.

"She might turn back like she did in January," Jeremy said. "Or go in toward the Cape like in March. But maybe."

He'd learned so much about Bertha because the shark spotting had messed up his dad's summer business last year. Most of Mr. Green's construction projects happened in the off-season, and then he took snorkelers and scuba divers out on his boat in the summer. After Bertha, most people had been too scared to go on boat trips, so Jeremy had started doing research to prove that sharks were almost never a threat to humans.

And Annabelle had gotten swept up in his interest. It was fun to see the world through Jeremy's eyes—as a place where you could spot a problem and feel so certain you could fix it. And there was something that fascinated her about Bertha, this creature who was so big and terrifying and yet still barely old enough to go out and explore by herself. She imagined Bertha's shark parents reminding her to be safe before they let her go out to swim around on her own, and then worrying while she was away.

"How big do you think she is now?" Annabelle asked.

They were out of their neighborhood now, reaching

the marshy wildlife preserve. Seagulls squawked over-head, and a dragonfly hovered at the edge of the path.

Jeremy shook his head. "No way to know for sure un-less another shark tagger finds her. Maybe nine feet?"

Up ahead, the summer dad pulled off to the side to check the bike path map, and Jeremy and Annabelle rode past, up to the mostly hidden entrance for Bluff Point.

They locked their bikes at the rack in front of the dunes, where Mia's pink cruiser was waiting. As they walked onto the beach, Annabelle kicked off her flip-flops, letting her feet sink into the soft sand. The waves were bigger than usual, leaving hissing white foam after they'd broken, and the seals were out, some resting on the rocks and others bobbing up and down in the water. She took in a big, salty gulp of ocean air.

Mia wore a bright blue bikini and lay facedown on her towel, kicking her already tan legs up and down as she read something on her phone. Annabelle had the kind of fair skin that either burned or did nothing, and Jeremy did, too. But Mia could spend five minutes out in the sun and *boom*: Her olive skin was golden-tan. "One good thing about Greek genes," she'd told Anna-belle once.

She popped up and ran over to Annabelle and Jer-emy, spraying sand with every step. She looked like the old Mia right now, with her dark eyes all lit up. The Mia from sixth grade and even the first half of seventh, who made Annabelle a card on National Best Friend Day and painted Annabelle's nails team colors before all their big meets last summer.

But when she opened her mouth, it was second-half-of-seventh-grade Mia all the way.

"I did it! Nothing below an A-minus except art, which my parents couldn't care less about!"

The words pushed all the soothing, salty-fresh air out of Annabelle's lungs, but she told herself to be happy for her friend.

"My dad's taking me anywhere I want in August to celebrate!" Mia said. "I think I'm going to pick L.A."

Her family was one of the few year-round island families with enough money to afford the full Gray Island tuition *and* plan a trip across the country in honor of a report card. They lived up the coast from Annabelle and Jeremy, in a neighborhood full of vacation homes. They used to be summer people who lived in Boston the rest of the year, but they'd moved here full-time right around the same time Annabelle had. Mia's dad's company had moved their office, so he was going to work from home anyway, and her mom, who had grown up in California, missed being near the ocean all the time.

"Congrats," Jeremy said. "That's awesome."

Then he snuck a wrinkly-foreheaded look over at Annabelle, and her heart cannonballed to the bottom of her stomach.

Jeremy knew. It didn't matter how hard she had tried to hide it. Jeremy knew how stupid she was, and he felt sorry for her.

She was already sure Mia had figured it out, since Mia peeked at her papers and lingered in the doorway when teachers talked to her after class. But Jeremy never peeked or eavesdropped. He was in a different section for history, so he hadn't heard Mr. Derrickson say, "I can't teach you if you don't even *try*" loud enough for everybody to hear as he handed back a mostly blank quiz. And he was always busy with mathletes or sitting with his guy friends when she went to Ms. Ames's office or met her tutor at lunch.

"Um, yeah. That's really great!" Annabelle managed. "Good job!"

She walked over to Mia's towel and sat next to it without bothering to spread out her own. Jeremy plopped down on her other side, and then Mia lowered herself back down, too. A little ways away, a lifeguard blew his whistle and motioned for two kids who'd gone out too far to come back in.

"How'd you guys do?" Mia asked. "You met Mr.

Derrickson like a zillion times for history help, right, Annabelle? Did you do well?"

Annabelle focused on the seals that bobbed up and down in the water, out past where the lifeguards let swimmers go, waiting for their turn to sunbathe on the rocks.

"Um, yeah," she said. "I studied a lot. My grade was . . . eh."

She shrugged to show it didn't really matter and buried her toes in the sand.

"Aww, Annabelle." Mia put her arm around Annabelle's shoulders, and Annabelle squirmed away to pick up a rock. Pink quartz, it looked like.

"Mr. Derrickson's the worst," Mia said. "He seriously wants people to fail. He's, like, a Satanist who takes pleasure in making people suffer."

"You mean a sadist?" Jeremy asked.

Mia reached over Annabelle to flick him in the ear. She never really minded when Jeremy corrected her, though. She was confident enough in her own intelligence that it didn't shake her when she got a word wrong.

"The point is, he's a miserable person. And not a fair teacher. That short-answer section was ridiculous—we barely ever talked about any of that."

Mia talked faster and lower than she used to. In the spring, she'd joined the lacrosse team and become friends with all the prettiest, loudest eighth graders. She sounded just like them now, and she said everything like it was a fact, even when it wasn't.

"It was a really hard final," Jeremy agreed.

But it hadn't been *too* hard for Jeremy or Mia. Only for Annabelle.

Annabelle wiped the sand off the pink quartz rock and ran her fingers over its rounded end. Pink quartz, white quartz, and salt-and-pepper granite—those were the most common kinds of rocks on the island, because they could handle getting pounded by the waves. She'd learned that her first year at the Academy, in sixth-grade science.

When they did their unit on the island habitat, she'd had questions about everything: why there were so many of those three kinds of rocks, why the ocean looked blue in the morning and greenish by afternoon, why all of the beaches were bordered with dunes.

And her teacher, Mrs. Mattson, would tell her, "What a terrific question!" And Jeremy would say, "I've never stopped to think about that!" And for as long as she was in science class, she almost felt smart.

Mia took the rock to examine it, and then dropped it back in Annabelle's palm. "Hey, what are you guys doing tomorrow? Wanna play mini golf?"

"Okay, yeah," Annabelle said, willing her voice to sound happy.

Mini golf with Mia was the best because Mia came up with silly challenges, like making everybody crouch down and hit the ball pool-cue style, with the skinny end of their clubs. And this was what Annabelle had wanted all spring. No lacrosse girls for Mia to sit with at lunch while she had to meet her tutor. No video-game-obsessed guys from Jeremy's advanced math class to invite him back to their dorm rooms to beat the next level of something or other. All the boarding kids had gone back to Boston and Connecticut and New Hampshire and New York, and now she and Mia and Jeremy could go back to being Annabelle, Mia, and Jeremy again, like last summer.

Annabelle had friends at school, too, but she wasn't around that much since she spent so much time studying and swimming. They were always nice to her when she was there, but she never got the impression that they missed her all that much when she wasn't.

She slid off her tank top, and Mia glanced at her black suit—the same one she'd been wearing the other day when Connor Madison had stared—and then looked away fast.

Back in the spring, Mia's mom had taken the two of them shopping in Boston, and they'd tried on the same striped shirt. On Mia, it had looked like a regular T-shirt. But when Annabelle had stepped out of the dressing room, Mia's mom had said, *"Va-va-voom! Honey, I don't think you can wear that shirt to school!"* Mia had rolled her eyes and told her mom to stop making a big deal out of nothing. But she'd frowned at her own reflection in a way that told Annabelle she didn't really think it was nothing. Now she was frowning down at her bikini top the same way.

Annabelle was about to ask if anyone wanted to go in the water when Mia said, "Hey, so what's the deal with genius camp, Jer?"

Jeremy's cheeks filled in with pink and he tried to brush away the hair that used to fall to his eyebrows before he'd gotten it cut. "I guess it's happening."

"Genius camp?" Annabelle repeated.

Jeremy reached behind her to flick Mia, but Mia pulled away so he only flicked air.

"That's not what it's called. It's an enrichment thing at a college in Boston for a few weeks. It starts next month. Samir's going, too."

Samir was Jeremy's closest guy friend at the Academy, and he lived in Massachusetts when he wasn't at school.

"It's kind of expensive, so I wasn't sure if I could go, but there was this scholarship thing, so . . ."

He trailed off, and Annabelle squeezed the pink quartz rock, hoping that would balance out the way her throat squeezed up and made it hard to breathe.

What about us? she wanted to say. *What about coming to Bluff Point every week and sharing a large cup at the Creamery—half peanut butter cup and half double-chocolate chunk—and going back to the Cape Cod shark museum like last summer to find out more about Bertha?*

But what came out was "What . . . what about summer swim team?"

Jeremy let out a little laugh as he ran his fingers over the top of his short hair. "I think the team will manage without me."

"Maybe," Mia said in her loud new lacrosse-girl voice. "But who will judge our amazing pool handstand competitions and order too many fries at the snack bar so we can steal the extras?"

"Those aren't extras!" Jeremy protested.

Annabelle made herself laugh along with them, but the sound came out shrill, like the bark of those bobbing seals who wanted their turn on the rocks.

Jeremy stood and brushed the sand off his legs, careful to step far enough away that it didn't hit Annabelle and Mia. "Wanna swim?"

Mia flopped back on her towel and picked up her phone. "You guys go. I need to text Reagan back."

Reagan was one of Mia's lacrosse friends who had just finished eighth grade. She was the loudest girl on the whole team, and she cursed and made fun of people in a way that she pretended was silly but always felt mean. Annabelle hadn't been that sorry to see her go back to Connecticut.

"She's super bored at home," Mia said. "I'm telling her she should visit so we can give her the true Gray Island experience!"

The true Gray Island experience. Like Mia had given Annabelle after they met at an Academy welcome event before sixth grade. Since Mia had come to Gray Island every summer for years, she'd already known that you could watch movies on the beach on Thursday nights in August, and that the Creamery's cookies were half price after five, and that the burger shack by the light-house had the best fish and chips and the best sunset views. She'd made it seem like having Annabelle with her made all of her favorite summer things even more fun. But maybe now, having Annabelle with her wasn't enough anymore.

Annabelle squeezed the pink quartz rock again—harder this time—before she buried it in the sand. Jeremy held a hand out to help her up, but she didn't take it. She pushed herself off the ground, shed her shorts, and bolted for the ocean, fighting the pull of the sand with every step.

Jeremy had almost caught up by the time the sand turned cool and mushy at the edge of the water, but she didn't stop. He liked to ease in a little at a time, and she liked to get in fast. She kept running, splashing cold, salty water up her arms and legs. Then she saw a big wave coming right at her, so she dove under and stayed there, beneath the surface, until it crested and rolled in to shore.

That was the thing about the ocean, even when it was rough: Even the most powerful waves passed if you stayed under for long enough, and Annabelle could hold her breath for ages thanks to swimming.

When she finally came up for air, she tried to imagine herself diving beneath everything she couldn't face thinking about—those Cs on her report card, the look on her mom's face, Jeremy leaving in July, and Mia still choosing Reagan over her when Reagan wasn't even here. It didn't really work, though.

Chapter 4

When Annabelle and Jeremy got dropped off at the pool the next day, the older team's practice was ending and Mia was already there, standing with a bunch of other girls from the middle school team. She was telling a story in her loud, low voice that made everyone look over to see what she was saying.

Annabelle wasn't sure how she did it. Mia was always in the middle of things at school, too, even though she missed everything at night and some things on the weekends, when she was at home instead of in the dorms. And lately, swim team was the same way.

Most of the other kids on the North Shore Sands summer team went to the public school, and they were always talking about stuff that happened at school and making jokes about Academy kids, with their expensive clothes and hyphenated last names and the way they took up the whole sidewalk when they went into town. But whenever they did that, Mia would say something funny or give someone a compliment and *boom*: The Academy jokes would stop, and everybody would circle around her.

Annabelle was still watching Mia as she started for the locker room, and she almost walked right into the strong, tan chest of a guy wearing only a navy-blue racing suit. She stopped short, stumbling, and then two hands reached out to steady her.

Connor Madison. His fingers sizzled against her bare shoulders.

"I'm—I'm sorry," Annabelle stuttered, but Connor grinned at her.

"Not a problem, Hummingbird. I like it when people almost run into me. Keeps me on my toes."

Most people had stopped using her old nickname by last summer, once she'd hit a growth spurt that had left her towering over half the boys. But Annabelle liked that Connor still called her that. It felt special, coming from him.

"Oh, um, okay," she said, even though he was obviously kidding.

But she couldn't focus on how silly she sounded because Connor's hands were so warm on her shoulders, and his blond hair had brighter blond streaks in the front from the sun like she always wished her own dirty-blond hair would get, and his eyes were so, so green. Almost as bright as her mom's birthstone, peridot. Which Mom thought was "garish," but what did Mom know.

The tips of Connor's ears were sunburned, and the skin at the tops were peeling a tiny bit. Annabelle wanted to touch them, even though the idea of touching dead skin should be disgusting. Mia's cousin, who'd never stopped texting with her boyfriend when she'd visited last summer, had told Mia and Annabelle that when you really, really like somebody, that changes how you see them, like how 3-D glasses change the way you see a movie. That's probably the kind of thing she was talking about—not being grossed out by somebody's dead ear skin.

Annabelle glanced back over at Mia, but Mia was still completely absorbed in whatever she was saying. When she'd texted Mia about what Connor had said to Jordan the other day after she'd gotten out of the pool, Mia had only texted back an open-mouth cat emoji. She couldn't tell if it was supposed to be a *Whoa, that's amazing! Maybe Connor's into you!* excited cat or a sort-of-surprised but not super-impressed one or what.

"I hear you're ready to crush all those under-fourteen records this summer, huh?" Connor asked, and Annabelle's heart sped up.

He *had*? Had he actually participated in a conversation about Annabelle and her swimming?

"I'm gonna try," she said, and that made him laugh for some reason. She liked the sound so much, she wanted to make him laugh again. "I think your old under-fourteen boys' backstroke one's safe for another summer, though."

"Whew," he said, pretending to wipe sweat off his forehead. "You're not gonna try to take down all the guys' ones, too?"

"Madison!" somebody called, and he turned his head to reply.

It didn't feel like their conversation had officially ended, but Annabelle wasn't sure if she should leave or wait around or what.

Before she could decide, Elisa Price came out of the girls' locker room with Jeremy's older sister, Kayla.

"It's my favorite under-fourteen swimmer!" Elisa said.

"Mine too, but don't tell Jer," Kayla joked.

Annabelle giggled but wasn't quite sure what to say. She always *used* to know what to say around Kayla, even though Kayla was older. When Annabelle, Mia, and Jeremy had started sixth grade, Kayla had been in ninth, and she'd been full of advice about which teachers were strict and which weekend events were worth going back to campus for. And she'd always acted like she really liked Annabelle and Mia.

One time she'd even told Annabelle what a rough time Jeremy had had in fifth grade, with some other kids picking on him, and how happy she was that he'd found a friend as nice as Annabelle, who appreciated how fun and smart and interesting he was.

But then as the year went on, Kayla had stopped going out of her way to talk to them quite so much, and she'd gotten thinner and thinner and started wearing big, thick sweaters even when it wasn't that cold. And last year, she'd missed the whole summer swim season to go to a program on the mainland for teens with eating disorders. Everything was a lot better now, but Annabelle was never sure whether she was supposed to say anything about being glad Kayla was okay now or act like she didn't know anything had happened or what.

"Hey, so I wasn't the only one you impressed the other day when you were swimming like there was a shark after you," Elisa said.

Kayla gave Annabelle a little inside-joke smile. They both knew that if Jeremy had heard that, he'd launch into a tirade about how unlikely it was that a shark would ever be "after Annabelle," unless she was on a surfboard and the shark mistook her for a turtle.

"Coach Colette asked me about you," Elisa went on. "She was practically salivating about how she'll get to coach you once you're fourteen, because she thinks your technique's so good."

Connor finished his other conversation and turned back, slinging one arm around Elisa's shoulders and the other arm around Kayla's.

"What's that now? Who's salivating?"

Elisa shook her head. "You're like a dog that perks up when someone says the word *food*. If anybody says anything that could in any way be twisted around to sound inappropriate, there you are."

Connor let out a puppy-like yip. "But a cute dog, right?"

Then he swung his long, muscly arms off the girls' shoulders.

"Gotta run. See ya, ladies," he said. "Have a good practice, HB."

Annabelle's heart swelled. A nickname for her nickname!

He gave all three of them a little salute and started to go. Annabelle waved at him like a little kid, closing her hand and then opening it, before she caught herself and pinned her arm behind her back.

That was definitely a super-excited-open-mouth-cat-emoji kind of interaction she and Connor had just had. She hoped Mia had seen some of it so they could talk later about what it had meant.

Elisa and Kayla said goodbye, and Jeremy came out of the guys' locker room all ready for practice. He stopped when he saw that Annabelle was still holding her bag and wearing her clothes over her suit.

"What, did you get lost?" he joked.

Connor turned his head before he reached his friends and saluted Annabelle again. Just in time, she remembered to straighten her posture and bend one leg a tiny bit, because Mia said that's what models do, to make their legs look thinner.

"Annabelle?" Jeremy said. "Hello?"

It took her a second to realize he was still there, waiting for her to respond.

When practice ended, Mitch was sitting at one of the tables, still wearing his collared shirt and dress pants from work. He always got to practice before it ended if he could. He wanted to make sure he and Coach Eric were on the same page with Annabelle's training.

But today, Coach Colette was with him, her clipboard balanced on the edge of the table.

Annabelle dried off with her purple towel and wrapped it around her, twisting it so nobody could see her name, which was stitched into one end in babyish, sea-green letters thanks to Mom, who would monogram Annabelle's underwear if she could.

"Meet you back out here after we change?" Jeremy asked.

He had just rubbed his towel over his hair, so it stuck up in spikes. Mia would probably come over to smooth them down any second, and then Jeremy would yank on her ponytail to get her back.

"Hey, Bananabelle!" Mitch called. "Come on over! Coach Colette wants to talk to you."

Jeremy raised his eyebrows, and the red indents from his goggles went up with them.

"Sorry," Annabelle said. "I guess I might be a little while."

Jeremy was really only on the swim team because Kayla swam and his mom wanted him to do something other than read and mess around on his computer in the summer. He was always the first person to congratulate Annabelle when she won a race, but sometimes, if he'd finished last in his own race, his smile didn't latch into place when he told her good job. And when a coach wanted to talk to *him* after practice, it was to tell him what he was doing wrong on his flip turns.

But he smoothed down his own hair spikes and shrugged. "That's okay. I'll wait for you and Mitch in the parking lot."

"You owe me a talking-animal video," she reminded him. At least that might give him something to look for while he waited.

She'd sent one to cheer him up a few weeks ago, when he'd gotten sick and missed the end-of-year school trip to Boston to see a show. They'd been sending them back and forth ever since, because who *didn't* need adorable animals with funny voiceovers in their lives? Their favorites were the ones that had actors' really serious, deep voices dubbed in as animals swatted each other or chased each other around.

"I'll see what I can do," he said, and Annabelle went to join Mitch and Colette.

"Hear you had a great practice today, kiddo," Mitch said.

"She sure did," Colette agreed. "You've got a lot of potential, Annabelle. Your power is impressive for your size. Especially on the butterfly."

Annabelle glanced at Colette's toned arms and shoulders. Maybe that's what her shoulders would look like someday. She already had long arms and legs that propelled her across the pool, but her limbs hadn't filled out with obvious muscle yet.

Mitch always said it was a good thing that Annabelle hadn't peaked yet, physically, because she'd be even faster when she did. Annabelle hoped that when she *did* peak, her body would look a lot like Colette's. People talked about how hot Colette was: pretty *and* strong. Annabelle wanted people to talk about her like that, too.

"I'm wondering what you think about the possibility of swimming up with us this summer," Colette said. "We could use some extra speed, especially on the relay teams. We have a chance at making it to the Labor Day Invitational, and you could really help make that happen."

Annabelle's heart jumped around in her chest as if she'd just beaten her fastest time in the 100-meter fly. Last year was the closest the North Shore Sands fourteen-and-up team had ever come to making the Labor Day Invitational, but they'd only finished fourth in the league, behind one other team from the island and two from the Cape. Only the top two teams in the league got to go.

Colette wanted her to be on the older team with all those high school swimmers, even though she was only thirteen?

"What do you think?" Colette asked again.

Annabelle imagined swimming the fly leg on a medley relay team with Elisa on freestyle. All the older girls high-fiving her after they won a big race—the race that got them into the Invitational. Connor Madison reaching down to hug her. Picking her up and spinning her around in the air, even, with everybody watching.

"I . . . I think that could be good." Annabelle's voice came out little-girl soft, so she cleared her throat and tried again. "I'd like that."

"We have to run the idea past Annabelle's mom, of course. But this sounds like a terrific opportunity!" Mitch said.

He sounded even happier than when he'd finally fixed up his little sailboat enough to get it out on the bay last summer, and it felt so good to be the one who could make him that happy.

Colette nodded. "Of course."

Annabelle practically skipped to the car, where Jeremy was waiting. Because if she could help the high school team get to the Labor Day Invitational? Then Jeremy wouldn't look at her with his forehead crinkled up with pity, and Mia wouldn't say, "Aww, Annabelle," and even Mom might see that doing well at swimming could be as important as doing well at school. And if Connor Madison kept looking at her the way he'd been looking at her?

Then it wouldn't matter if Reagan visited Mia and Jeremy left in July and this summer wasn't like last summer. Then this summer would be *better* than last summer. Than *any* summer.

Chapter 5

The good thing was, Mom said yes right away when Annabelle asked about swimming up on the high school team. "As long as you stick to the summer reading schedule and don't miss tutoring."

Annabelle didn't see her regular tutor during the summer, but as soon as Mom had seen her report card, she'd lined up Janine, who had graduated from the Academy two years ago and was home from college. Janine was supposed to help Annabelle get through her summer reading books and get a head start on the history textbook for next year, since Mr. Derrickson was going to be her teacher again.

"School comes first, even in the summer," Mom added, her voice way too loud for how close together they were sitting.

They were eating dinner out on the deck, Annabelle's favorite part of the house. Before they'd moved in, they'd had to replace half of the wood because it was rotting. At first, the new parts weren't weathered yet, so the new cedar planks and shingles were smooth and light brown instead of rough and dark gray like everything else. Mom had hated the way the new parts didn't match. But Annabelle had liked looking at the floor of the deck, where a new piece of wood lay right smack next to an old one. Same length, same width, and from the same kind of tree, but a completely different color and texture.

Slowly, the new ones were getting closer and closer to matching the old, and there was something comforting about watching them change a little bit at a time and knowing that she'd been there for all the windy winter days and sunny summer ones that had weathered them.

"You know that's the deal, right?" Mom asked, and Annabelle sighed.

"I already told you I'd do the work."

Mom took a bite of salad and dabbed the corner of her mouth with her red cloth napkin, which matched the red gingham place mats she'd set out and the red jar for the citronella candle that burned in the middle of the table, keeping mosquitoes away.

"Then I think this will be a really good thing for you, Belle."

"It'll be good for the rest of the team, too," Mitch said, reaching over to ruffle Annabelle's hair. "I've watched them, Kim. None of them can swim the fly as fast as our powerhouse here."

Mom squeezed Annabelle's hand. "You've always been our little fish. Ever since those first lessons your dad took you to, back at the Y in New Jersey when you were so tiny. And I know you've worked hard, too. It's wonderful, honey."

At the edge of the deck, a firefly lit up—the very first one Annabelle had seen this season. For a moment, Annabelle felt *herself* light up inside, too. Mom *was* proud of her for swimming, even if she couldn't rattle off her best time for the 100-meter fly like Mitch could.

But then Mom's eyes got all twinkly as if she were about to say something really great, except what she said was "So in other news, I talked to Mrs. Sloane today! I set up an appointment for us to meet on July 10."

A minute.

That's how long they spent talking about the best thing to happen to Annabelle for as long as she could remember. Maybe not even.

"Why?" Annabelle asked.

Mrs. Sloane was the head of the middle school at Gray Island Academy. When Annabelle had first interviewed there, she'd closed her office door and told

Annabelle how hard she'd have to work. "To stay afloat." That's how she'd put it, and Annabelle had pictured the little kids at the pool, paddling their arms and legs as they learned to tread water.

"It's just . . . You did your part, Belle, that whole last quarter," Mom said. "You worked as hard as anybody could."

"And I still did badly," Annabelle finished.

Mom winced, but she didn't correct her.

Next door, the two little Bennett girls, Julia and Kelsey, burst outside. Julia was blowing bubbles and Kelsey carried a blue plastic bucket that rattled as she ran after her big sister. Mrs. Bennett followed them out and closed the screen door.

"Hi there!" she called. "Nice night, isn't it?"

"Beautiful," Mom agreed.

Annabelle waved at the girls, and Kelsey ran over. She stared down into her bucket, picked out a ridged white shell, and handed it to Annabelle. "Here."

"Thanks, Kelsey," Annabelle said, but Kelsey was off, running back down the deck steps and into her yard, where her sister had stopped blowing bubbles and started spinning in circles.

Annabelle turned the shell over in her hand and put it down next to her plate. Faint pink lines striped the inside, and it was almost whole except for a chip at the top.

Mom took a sip of her water, then set the glass down and rubbed her fingertips against her temples. "I don't want you to have to go through it all again—what you went through this spring. All that work and then all that disappointment."

But what was the alternative? Not working as hard so the disappointment wouldn't be so big?

In the Bennetts' yard, Kelsey squealed as Julia chased her. Mitch's knife creaked against his plate as he cut himself a bite of grilled chicken.

"Mrs. Sloane said she'd look back at your learning plan to make sure the school is following through on all your accommodations," Mom said. "Maybe you could use your notes for some of your tests so you wouldn't have to memorize so much. And maybe you should be getting extra time for little quizzes, too. Not just the bigger assessments."

Annabelle cringed. It was embarrassing enough to have people ask where she'd been when she took extra time for tests. If she got to take out her notes when everybody else didn't and left the room for extra time on every tiny quiz, too? Ugh.

Mitch spoke up. "Well, I think this could be a good opportunity to strategize. Come up with a new action plan for next year, right?"

Those were typical Mitch words: *opportunity* and *strategize* and *action plan*. The whole reason they'd moved to Gray Island was that Mitch had found an opportunity to capitalize on—someone from his old job had told him there weren't any finance people on the island, so if the year-round families wanted help investing their money or making business plans for their stores or planning for their retirement, they had to go to the mainland.

"Right!" Mom agreed. "Maybe Mrs. Sloane will have suggestions we haven't thought of. Things that have helped other students in the past."

"Maybe," Annabelle said.

Or maybe Mrs. Sloane would say she wasn't really Gray Island Academy material after all.

She cleared her throat. "What . . . what if Mrs. Sloane says they don't want to keep giving me financial aid?"

Mom and Mitch both had successful businesses now, but Mitch had two daughters from when he was married before, and they were both in college. Annabelle knew their tuitions cost a lot. She was pretty sure Mom and Mitch couldn't afford to pay any more of her Academy tuition than they already did.

And if she had to start over at public school, then everyone would know she hadn't been smart enough to handle the Academy. And the other girls from swim team would say things like "Oh, you decided our school was good enough for you after all?" And they'd say it like they were joking, but they wouldn't be, really.

Mom set down her forkful of chicken and pushed her plate away.

"That's not going to happen," she said.

And that was that. Conversation over.

Chapter 6

After dinner, Annabelle shuffled through the mail that Mitch had left on the table in the hallway. The official copy of her report card should be coming any day now, and she hated the idea of Mom picking up the fancy version that was always printed on thick cream-colored paper with the Academy logo as if it were some keepsake to treasure.

But there wasn't anything from the Academy in the stack. It was mostly catalogs and junk and then a small square envelope that peeked out from underneath a bill.

The return address said Boston, and there was her own name, written in handwriting she hadn't seen in ages. The big round *A*. The *n*s that joined together, as if they were holding hands. Her last name, Wilner—the name only *she* still had now, since Mom had taken Mitch's when they got married—written with a big, pointy *W* and an *r* that flattened out into a line.

She grabbed the envelope and bolted up to her room, her heart pounding against her rib cage as her feet pounded against the stairs.

Her fingers shook hard enough that she gave herself a paper cut when she tore the letter open. A white line appeared on her finger, and after a second, it filled up with a round red blob. Some of the blood stained the corner of the paper, and she sucked on her fingertip to make the bleeding stop.

Dear Annie, the letter started.

She had almost forgotten that he called her that, which was ridiculous. It hadn't been *that* long.

I've wanted to be in touch with you for a long time, but now that I am writing, I don't know quite what to say. I'm sorry, for starters. I'm sorry for being absent and nothing like the kind of father I always planned to be. I think of you often and will love you always. I'm doing much better now. I moved to Boston with a friend, and if you ever want to see me, my door will always be open. Please write back any time you want

to. I would love to hear from you, and I miss you
every single day.

Love, Dad

Annabelle read the letter twice, and she didn't even notice that tears were streaming down her face until the words began to blur. She grabbed a bunch of tissues from the box on her bedside table, wiped off her face, and wrapped one around the cut on her finger. Then she read the note a third time, focusing on the big take-aways and lingering questions, the way Ms. Ames always told her to do at school.

Dad was in Boston, only a couple of hours away. He had moved there with a friend. A girlfriend?

Could he have moved closer on purpose? Because he wanted to be near Annabelle?

That idea was way too earthshakingly enormous to consider. She buried the letter under the stack of school notebooks and binders that still sat on her desk and picked up Kelsey Bennett's shell, which she hadn't even realized she'd brought upstairs.

She had a shell lamp with a clear glass base on the nightstand next to her bed. Mitch had given it to her when they first moved to the island, and she and Mom had walked up and down the beach, searching for the best shells to fill it up with. Whole ones, without broken edges.

Except it turned out to be impossible to find enough unbroken shells to fill up the entire lamp. Eventually, they'd both gotten frustrated, so Mitch had found the rest and set it up. Annabelle had figured he knew some special, protected spot where all the shells stayed whole, but then last spring, she'd finally asked him where he'd gone.

"I bought them at one of the gift shops in town," he'd admitted. "You wanted all of the shells to be perfect, and there was no way to find enough."

You wanted all of the shells to be perfect.

Had she really wanted that? Or was it Mom who'd thought her shell lamp wouldn't be beautiful if it was filled with broken shards?

She took off the shade, unscrewed the cap on top of the base, and set Kelsey's at the top, turned so she could see the chipped edge.

Then she sat there on her bed, staring at that broken shell and remembering the way Mom had pushed away her plate when Annabelle had asked what would happen if she lost her financial aid. As if just the possibility made her lose her appetite.

She wondered what her dad would say about her terrible report card. He wouldn't have gasped like Mom had. He hadn't been a good student—he'd told her that tons of times.

But he had no idea she needed accommodations and learning plans and tutors. None of them had known, back when they still lived in New Jersey. Back then, she didn't read the highest-level books, which had letters from the end of the alphabet on their spines, like *T*, or *U*, or *V*. But she didn't read the very lowest-level ones, either.

Mom had always said she'd be able to read at a higher level if only she'd practice more. Build her "reading muscles," in addition to her swimming ones. Mom kept giving her paperback copies of the books she'd loved when she was a kid and waiting for the "reading bug" to bite, but then Dad would say it still hadn't bitten him and he was fine.

Except he *hadn't* been fine, it turned out.

But maybe now he was?

Maybe now he was a bit like Kelsey's shell—chipped at the edge from everything that had gone wrong but mostly whole? Mostly okay?

If you ever want to see me. That's what his letter said.

But *did* she actually want to see him?

Was she a terrible daughter—a terrible *person*—if she didn't?

She opened the top of her shell lamp and turned Kelsey's shell around. She wasn't so sure she could handle looking at the chipped part anymore after all.

Chapter 7

The next day, Mitch drove Annabelle to her first high school team practice.

"Knock 'em dead, kiddo," he said when he pulled up to the curb.

Then he blew her a kiss, which she caught. It was a little bit silly, the kiss-and-catch routine, but they'd always done it. Ever since they'd first met, when Annabelle was in third grade. Her parents' divorce was just final then, and Dad lived in an apartment where there was almost no furniture and everything was white: the walls, the carpets, the fans that spun from the ceilings, even the fridge and kitchen cabinets. Mom said he wasn't really up for decorating. But he was still up for seeing Annabelle most Saturdays back then.

One Saturday when he was busy, Mom had made a big thing about taking Annabelle to brunch with her new "friend," and the friend turned out to be Mitch. There was a make-your-own waffle station at the restaurant, and Mitch made a whipped cream smiley face on Annabelle's waffle, with blueberries inside the eyes and strawberries for the mouth. And he made Mom laugh so hard she snorted a little bit, and then she covered her whole face with her napkin until he reached over and squeezed her hand.

After they ate, Mom and Annabelle went to their car and Mitch went to his. But before he opened the door, he blew two kisses: one to Mom in the front seat, and one to Annabelle in the back. He'd been doing it ever since.

But Annabelle suddenly realized: She couldn't even remember how she used to say goodbye to her dad. Before he "dropped out of the picture," as her mom always put it. Had they hugged? Kissed on the cheek?

Dad had been "in the picture" for way more years than he'd been out of it. They must have said goodbye thousands of times. How did she just not know?

She caught herself biting her bottom lip and heard Mom's voice in her head saying, "Honey, don't bite." A group of older girls she sort of recognized laughed as they walked in from the parking lot.

One of them had *driven* there, she realized. Some of her new teammates were old enough to *drive*. She paused inside the gate. It was hard enough to feel like she fit in with the other kids on the middle school team, with all their inside jokes from school and the way they imitated the boarding students from the Academy. How would she possibly fit in with high schoolers?

"Hey, Annabelle!" Doug, the guy at the sign-in desk, said. "The pool's over there!"

Annabelle forced out a laugh and made herself start moving again. Head up, shoulders back. Carrying herself with confidence, like Mitch would tell her to.

When she came out of the locker room wearing her suit, Connor was joking around with a bunch of other guys and he didn't notice her. But Kayla waved her over, and then Colette gathered everybody around, and suddenly practice was starting.

Annabelle's hands shook as she twisted her hair into a bun and stretched her swim cap over it, and it took three tries to get her goggles over her head. But as she pushed off the wall and glided through her first warm-up lap, she was able to block out the whole world each time she put her head underwater. And since she couldn't hear anything except the muffled splashing of her own arms and legs, she forgot about what it meant that Colette had assigned her to lane 6 with girls going into ninth grade who were okay swimmers but not great, and she forgot how fast the girls in lane 1 were probably swimming, and she even almost forgot that Connor Madison was there, only a few lanes away, with his long arms slicing through the surface of the water.

After warm-ups were finished and they'd done some faster laps, it was time to practice the medley relay.

"We've been needing a strong butterfly to round out our team," Colette said as she walked Annabelle over to the end of the pool where Kayla and Elisa were standing with a pretty summers-only girl who'd been new to the team last year. "We've got Kayla on backstroke, Ruby on breaststroke, and Elisa on free. Ladies, do you all know Annabelle?"

"Of course!" Elisa said. "Welcome!"

And Kayla said, "Yay! It's so great you're here!"

"Yeah, seriously," Elisa agreed. "Ruby and I were on the relay last year, and we almost never won a race. Right, Rubes? We need you!"

Annabelle was starting to relax a little bit, but then she noticed how Ruby was sort of examining her, with her eyebrows raised and her lips pressed together.

Annabelle knew she didn't look like a high school butterflyer. She was taller than the other middle school girls, but she wasn't as tall as Elisa or Ruby. Her chest and hips curved, but her shoulders were narrow and her arm and leg muscles only rippled when she flexed them.

Elisa's and Ruby's arms, calves, and thighs were thicker than Annabelle's and obviously strong. Kayla's were, too. She'd gotten so, so thin when she was sick, but now she was closer to her size from before. They all looked like swimmers in a way that Annabelle didn't.

"Congrats on joining the team," Ruby said. "What grade are you going into? Seventh?"

Her voice was sugary sweet and too high-pitched—the kind of voice people used to talk to little kids.

"Eighth," Annabelle said.

"Aww, I loved eighth grade!"

Kayla messed with her goggles strap, and Elisa was still smiling her friendly smile, as if she thought Ruby's sweetness was genuine. Maybe Annabelle was being oversensitive?

"All right, ladies. There'll be plenty of time for socializing later. Let's get going," Colette said.

Kayla jumped back into the pool, since backstroke goes first, and Ruby lined up by the blocks to go second.

Annabelle had been swimming the fly leg of the medley relay for ages, so she was used to being third in the order, after back and breast. But Kayla and Ruby were a lot faster than anybody she'd ever been on a relay team with. Before she knew it, Ruby was already halfway done with her leg and quickly approaching.

Annabelle glanced over to the end of the pool, where Connor stood with a bunch of other almost-sophomores. Her legs shook a little as she stood up on the starting block.

"You got this," Elisa said quietly. "Just do your thing."

Annabelle nodded and repeated that in her head. *Just do your thing.*

There were lots and lots of things she couldn't do well, but swimming was one thing she could.

So she took her three breaths and dove in as soon as Ruby's hands touched the edge. She had too much adrenaline at first and was wasting energy, rising up too far out of the water on her first few strokes.

When she took a test at school, that buzz of nerves overtook her muscles and then her brain until she couldn't think at all. But now the buzz shrunk down smaller and smaller, as if she were turning down the volume on music one notch at a time. The water stopped fighting her and there it was: that feeling she loved. Of knowing exactly what she was doing with every stroke. Of being completely in control of her body.

When she raised her head for a breath, she was dimly aware of the usual background noises—laughter, low voices, splashing. A couple of times, she even made out the sound of someone cheering her name.

She sped to the end of the pool, turned, and flew back the other way, her muscles firing.

And when she picked up her head, she could hear two things: the splash of Elisa's arms hitting the water to start her freestyle leg and applause. Loud cheers, coming from everybody on the team. Ruby was clapping along, and Kayla gave Annabelle a high five. And Connor Madison was right there in the front of the pack, letting out a giant whistle. For *her*.

Chapter 8

When practice ended, Annabelle felt better than she had in ages.

Visualize yourself achieving your goals. That was another thing Mitch always said. He visualized silly things, like pulling the car into an empty parking spot if they drove into town for ice cream when everything was mobbed with summer people, and important things, like getting the newspaper to run a story about Mom's new event-planning business at the start of last summer.

"We've been needing a strong butterfly to round out the team," Colette had said.

"We almost never won last year," Elisa had said.

And Annabelle knew exactly what to visualize.

She pictured herself reaching the wall ahead of the competition on her leg of the medley relay at the Labor Day Invitational, after she'd helped the team win their entire league. The cheers would be ten times as loud as today, and Kayla and Ruby would jump up and down and hug her as they all watched Elisa bring home the win.

Last year the relay team had almost never won. This year, Annabelle wanted to make sure they never lost. Then Mia and Jeremy and everyone else who had ever felt sorry for her would know that she didn't need their pity.

And even if her grades got worse and worse and she couldn't stay at the Academy, it wouldn't be quite so humiliating that she hadn't been smart enough to make it there. People would think, *Sure, she isn't the smartest, but have you seen that girl swim?* When all Mom's friends and all the summer people whose parties she planned asked about Annabelle, Mom wouldn't be able to tell them that Annabelle went to the Academy anymore. But she could tell them, *My daughter led her high school relay team to a championship as an eighth grader!*

As Annabelle walked to the locker room, she felt so good that she didn't even need to remind herself to hold her head up and her shoulders back. Until she saw Mia.

Mia stood over by the snack bar tables, with Jeremy next to her. She had her hands on her hips and her lips twisted to one side.

Oh no.

Annabelle had meant to call Mia last night to tell her about switching to the high school team, but then she'd seen the letter from Dad. She'd completely forgotten.

"You're not swimming with us anymore?" Mia asked, and it wasn't her lacrosse-girl voice she used right now. Mia could shrug off a lot of things that would have bothered Annabelle, but when something upset her, it *really* upset her. And right now she sounded as upset as she had last winter when her dad had gotten stuck in Chicago on her birthday because of a snowstorm, so they'd had to postpone the special dad-and-daughter birthday breakfast they had every year.

"I'm so sorry I didn't tell you," Annabelle said. "It all happened really fast. But I'll still see you guys all the time! I'll cheer you on at meets and stuff."

"Okay. Yeah, that definitely makes up for ditching us and not even saying anything about it."

And now the lacrosse-girl voice was back, but extra loud and low and with a really, really sharp edge. As sharp as one of the X-Acto knives they weren't allowed to use without supervision in the art room.

Next to Mia, Jeremy stared down at his flip-flops, which were getting a little too small. His big toes reached the very end. Annabelle tried to catch his eye to figure out if he'd told Mia that he already knew she was moving up to the high school team, but he wouldn't look up.

Annabelle took her three breaths. Mia was jealous, she told herself.

She was probably as jealous as Annabelle had been when their Spanish teacher had asked Mia to be a peer tutor, since her accent was so good. Or when Jeremy had gotten to move up to ninth-grade math when they were only seventh graders.

And it probably hurt Mia's feelings that Annabelle hadn't said anything to her about the high school team the way it had hurt Annabelle's feelings that time Reagan said something about Mia's crush on that eighth grader Alex Jones before Annabelle had known about it. Or else Mia was disappointed because, even though she didn't always act like it, she'd been looking forward to hanging out with Annabelle all summer, too.

Annabelle could make her feel better, though. She could make things right again if she could figure out the right thing to say.

"Um, Mitch can't pick me up for a while. Maybe I can stick around while you guys practice and then get him to take us all to the Creamery."

"Sounds good to me," Jeremy said, and Mia shrugged.

"I bet he'll get us half-price cookies to take home, too," Annabelle added. "And maybe that guy will be working. The one Reagan said was flirting with you last time you guys went?"

Jeremy rolled his eyes, but Mia nodded.

"Okay, I'm in," she said, and her voice wasn't so sharp now. "I guess we better say goodbye to Annabelle the Swimming Phenomenal and go practice with the middle schoolers."

"I think you mean phenom," Jeremy told her. "Or phenomenon, maybe."

"Whatever," she said, sliding her arm through his. "Let's go, Dictionary Boy."

Jeremy shook his head. "That sounds like the dorkiest superhero in the history of the world."

"Cheerio!" Mia called over her shoulder in a fake British accent. That's what she used to say whenever she and Annabelle had to leave each other to go to different classes at school.

Annabelle had done it. They were okay. Or as okay as they had been for a while, anyway.

"Ta-ta!" she called back.

She settled in to watch her friends swim, her muscles the best kind of tired and her mind mostly calm. This was going to be good for her and Mia, if she had Kayla and Elisa and even Connor Madison to hang out with, the way Mia had all her other friends. If she didn't need Mia so much more than Mia needed her but they both made time for each other.

Things would be more even then, and everything went better in a friendship when things were even. She was sure of it.

Chapter 9

The meet on Friday was against South Shore, and South Shore was good. Last summer, their high school team had finished first on the island and second in the league, so they'd made it to the Invitational.

The middle school meet was first, and Annabelle got there early to cheer for Mia and Jeremy. But the longer she sat there, the more nervous she got.

Last year, the middle school team had lost to South Shore, but this year they won without her. Mia took Annabelle's spot as anchor on the freestyle relay and butterfly on the medley, and at the end of the meet, she collected high fives and hugs from everybody who usually rushed over to congratulate Annabelle.

"Awesome job!" the middle school team coach's voice boomed as he patted Mia's shoulder, and Annabelle's heart lurched.

Stop, she told herself. Compliments weren't like the equations they learned about in math class that had to stay balanced. There could be plenty to go around.

Mitch would say she should make herself think positive. "Believe to achieve" and all of that. So as she walked over to the end of the pool where the high school team gathered, she tried the visualization trick.

There. She saw herself at the Labor Day Invitational, touching the wall at the end of her medley relay leg ahead of the competition. Setting a team record. A league record, even.

Okay. Her next breath came in easier. She stopped to congratulate Mia and Jeremy and then joined the high school team.

Elisa waved and then twisted her thick curly hair back into a bun and pulled on her cap. She had so much hair that it made an extra big conehead shape in the back. Annabelle had heard her joke once that this was her version of practicing with a second suit on to get more drag, and someday she was going to cut off all of her hair and shave seconds off her racing times.

"You ready for this?" she asked Annabelle.

And then there was Connor, right next to Elisa.

"Of course she's ready," Connor said. "She's Hummingbird!"

Ruby was there, too, her reddish-brown hair still

straight and sleek around her shoulders. Annabelle's wavy blond hair only looked that perfect if she had her mom blow-dry it with a round brush, and she wondered if Ruby had blow-dried her hair just for these few minutes before the swim meet started. Ruby smiled, which made her face even prettier than usual.

Except then she said, "I really hope Annabelle's ready. I want to win the medley relay!"

"Yeah, we could definitely use those points," Connor agreed. "Last year South only beat us by three the second time we raced them."

Annabelle's heart rate picked up, racing even faster than it had during the hardest part of practice yesterday. And during warm-ups, she kept hearing Connor's voice in her head.

We could definitely use those points.

She couldn't hold on to the image of herself leading the team to a victory at the Invitational, but maybe that was too far away. Maybe she needed to start smaller and work her way up. She tried to imagine herself speeding across the pool today with the water giving way, but even inside her head, the swimmers on either side gained on her, and Ruby turned to Connor and said, *I told you she doesn't belong on a high school team.*

After warm-ups, Annabelle reached her arms over her head to stretch them out. Jeremy and Mia were across the pool, on the second row of the bleachers, and Mom and Mitch sat front and center. Mitch blew Annabelle a kiss and gave her a thumbs-up. Annabelle caught the kiss with her hand low around her stomach so nobody else would see.

"You good?" Elisa asked, and Annabelle must have nodded. "Then let's go line up. It's time."

There was another relay group from Annabelle's team and two teams from South Shore. She spotted the A group from South Shore immediately. They were jumping up and down, psyching each other up, and they were *huge*. Even Elisa was shorter than all but one of them. And the tallest girl with the giant shoulder muscles was probably their butterflyer.

Against middle schoolers, Annabelle had an advantage because of her height. But this girl had longer limbs than she did, and how could she compete with someone that strong?

Kayla and the other three backstrokers lowered themselves into the pool.

It doesn't matter who's swimming next to me, Annabelle told herself as she stretched her arms some more. She had to focus on what she could control. Swim her own race. That's what Mitch would tell her.

The buzzer went off, and Kayla and the three other swimmers pushed off the wall. Kayla's start wasn't great, and the two South Shore girls got out in front of her. A tiny part of Annabelle wanted Kayla to fall way behind, so if they lost it would be her fault. But that was terrible. Kayla was her friend!

Annabelle cheered as Kayla gained on the other girls a little at a time. By the time she was nearing the end of her swim, she'd passed one of them and was a split second behind the other.

Ruby dove in and came up for a breath a tiny bit ahead of the girl from the South Shore A team. Her stroke was quick and clean. Breaststroke was usually the slowest leg of the relay, but Ruby's pace was almost as fast as Kayla's. Next to Annabelle, the tall, strong butterflyer jumped up and down. "Let's go, let's go!" she shouted.

Pull ahead, Annabelle willed Ruby. *Give me some kind of lead.*

But the girl on South Shore was just as fast as Ruby. Annabelle looked again at the butterflyer next to her. The only way she had any chance of staying close to this girl was to get into the water faster. She could be quicker off the blocks and get more momentum under the water before they both surfaced to start their stroke.

Sometimes Annabelle could gain a whole body's length on the other swimmers with her entrance into the water. If she could do that, she could stay close enough to give Elisa a shot to win the race, even if the South Shore girl overtook her.

We could really use the points.

Annabelle stepped up onto the blocks. Her job was to help the team come in first or second in the league so they could make it to the Invitational. That's what Colette had told her. It would be almost impossible to do that if they couldn't beat South Shore.

Ruby was getting close now. A few strokes away. Now two. Now—

As Ruby extended her arms forward, Annabelle launched into the pool. She stayed under as long as she could, and when her head broke the surface, she knew she was ahead of everyone else. Her adrenaline pushed her forward as her head and shoulders shot out of the water—she didn't waste any energy popping up too high. She could feel the South Shore A team girl on her left, but she kicked even harder, and her turn was perfect.

The tall butterflyer gained on her, but Annabelle was *not* going to lose enough ground that Elisa didn't have a chance to win the race. She pushed harder than she ever had before—pull, kick, pull, kick—and she and the broad-shouldered girl touched the wall at the very same time.

In the next lane, the other team's best freestyle swimmer splashed into the water, and then Elisa was in, too.

Annabelle hoisted herself out of the pool, gulping for air. Kayla and Ruby stood behind the blocks. Kayla put her arm around Annabelle for a second, but she and Ruby barely even clapped when Elisa came up for breaths. Why weren't they cheering for real?

Maybe that was a middle school thing, to squeal and yell and wave your arms every time your teammate came up for air and could hear you? Except that the South Shore teams on either side of them were doing plenty of yelling.

Elisa was about even with the South Shore girl, swimming cleanly but not as powerfully as Annabelle had seen her swim before. And after she made her turn, she started losing ground.

"Come on, Elisa!" Annabelle called.

Elisa could go faster than this! Maybe she'd pulled a muscle on one of her early strokes? The B team girl from South Shore was almost even with her, and the rest of the South Shore team was shouting. But still, no one really cheered Elisa on.

The South Shore A girl touched the wall first. Then Elisa and the South Shore B girl, so close together that Annabelle couldn't tell who'd come in before the other.

The rest of the South Shore girls rushed the pool, but Kayla and Ruby stayed where they were. Elisa pushed herself up and out of the water, and she pulled her goggles up to wipe her eyes.

"We'll get them next time," Annabelle said. "You still swam fast."

And that's when the official approached to tell them. "North Shore Sands," he said. "You're disqualified for an early start on the butterfly leg."

But . . . butterfly leg?

That was Annabelle! She thought she'd timed it perfectly. Her big toe had still been touching the end of the block when Ruby had reached the wall. Hadn't it? She'd never been called for leaving early in any of her races. Never.

That's why Elisa hadn't swum her fastest. Elisa must have seen the line judge raise her flag. She'd had to swim her leg anyway, but she'd known from the beginning that it wouldn't count.

"It's okay," Ruby said. "It happens."

She patted Annabelle on the back before she walked away, but she probably only meant *It happens when you let middle school kids swim with the high school team.*

"We have lots more races left," Kayla added.

She gave Annabelle a quick hug, and Elisa leaned in to squeeze Annabelle's shoulder.

"You swam really well," Elisa told her.

But it didn't matter.

We could definitely use those points, Connor had said. And in her first medley relay, Annabelle hadn't earned the team any points at all.

Later in the meet, Annabelle swam the 100-meter fly and the anchor leg of the team's third-best freestyle relay team. The relay team came in fifth, so they didn't earn any points, either. She managed to earn some when she came in second to the really tall, strong girl in the fly, but when the final scores were tallied, her team had lost by five. Even more than they'd lost by last summer. With her on the team, they were *worse* than last year, not better.

After the meet, she sat between Elisa and Kayla. Usually, there was something satisfying about the way her muscles stung after a meet, but today her whole body just felt tired. Empty. She barely listened as Colette told them what they'd done well and what they needed to improve on, because she already knew what she needed to improve on. Not getting her whole relay team DQ'd.

When Colette finished, Kayla said, "You should come over tonight if you're free. It's TV and taco night, and

Jer's been moping around complaining how bored he is with Samir and them gone. You'd cheer him up."

But Annabelle couldn't imagine cheering anybody up when she felt this miserable. "Thanks, but I think I have family stuff," she said, and then she rushed over to Mom and Mitch. She didn't even check to see if Jeremy and Mia were still around waiting for her.

"Can we go?" she asked Mom.

Mom was in the middle of a conversation with some other parents, but she didn't object the way she usually would have, and she didn't remind Annabelle to say goodbye to all of the adults, calling them Mr. or Mrs. whatever, even though all the other island kids called one another's parents by first names.

On the way home, Mia sent Annabelle a text with a whole bunch of hearts, and Jeremy sent a video with giraffes head-butting each other. Annabelle managed to send hearts and a **thanks** back to Mia and an **LOL** to Jeremy, and then she put away her phone.

Mitch tried to talk about how Annabelle had lost some power on her kick in the 100-meter fly and she should make sure to extend her arms all the way forward, but she didn't really listen. She looked out the window as they passed those huge gray houses near the pool—the ones that had stood empty and dark in the off-season but were all lit up now, with fancy cars with out-of-state license plates in the driveways, and big grills uncovered on the side decks, and little kids running around in their bathing suits in the emerald-green yards. Those summer kids were always so happy when they were here on the island. So completely carefree.

Mom tried the old "You tried your hardest and that's what counts" line she usually only had to pull out for schoolwork, and Annabelle let out a short laugh. It didn't make her feel any better when Mom said it about swimming, either.

Chapter 10

On Monday, Mitch took an early lunch break and drove Annabelle and Jeremy to the pool before practice so he could help Annabelle do some extra work on her starts.

Annabelle meant to ask Mia to come, too. She told herself she was going to text Sunday afternoon, and then Sunday night, and then first thing when she woke up . . . but she just couldn't.

She sometimes got the feeling that Mia was . . . Not that she was *happy* when Annabelle didn't do well at something, exactly. But sort of always keeping track of which of them was ahead. And right now Annabelle was dragging way too far behind.

"Hey, so I know this is kind of weird to ask," Annabelle said when she and Jeremy walked up to the pool a few feet ahead of Mitch, who was on a work call. "But could you maybe not say anything to Mia about me asking you to come today?"

Jeremy's light brown eyebrows—a touch lighter than the rest of his hair—edged together. "Are you guys fighting or something?"

"No! We're fine. I just don't want to hurt her feelings, and I . . ." She wasn't sure how to explain it without sounding like she was criticizing Mia. "It was easier to just have you come, since you were right on our way to the pool, and she's way out in the other direction."

"Oh. Okay. Got it." He smiled, but it wasn't his usual smile. This one wobbled a little at the edges.

"Plus, I guess I kind of only wanted you," Annabelle blurted. "I knew you'd help, and you wouldn't make me feel bad."

And now Jeremy's smile spread for real.

Behind them, Mitch ended his call. "All right!" he said, catching up. "Let's practice those starts!"

So Annabelle stood up on the start blocks and Jeremy got in the pool, and then Mitch kept making Jeremy swim the last ten meters of a breaststroke leg, even though Jeremy never raced breast. Mitch called out instructions as Annabelle dove in over and over.

"You can go sooner!" he yelled when she came up for a breath on her fifth or sixth try. "Right as Jeremy stretches out toward the wall!"

But even though she'd been timing her entrances right for ages, today it felt impossible to start her dive as early as she was used to while making sure her toes still kissed the end of the block when Jeremy's fingers touched.

She'd always been able to leave early enough to get an advantage, but not so early she got flagged. But maybe she'd been cheating all along and only fourteen-and-up officials called it? Maybe now that she was swimming up with high schoolers, her advantage was gone?

Jeremy was out of breath as she passed him on the way back to the starting block. "I'm sorry," she said, but he shook his head.

"It's fine," he said, panting. "It's good for me to get extra practice."

He took his place ten meters from the end, and Annabelle stood back up on the blocks. She didn't usually mind the way the rough surface scratched the bottoms of her feet, but right now she couldn't stand the way it prickled, and she couldn't bear to watch Jeremy gasp for air as his head bobbed up and down in the water, like one of those seals at Bluff Point.

"You know what?" she said. "We need a break. Can we get some lunch, Mitch?"

Mitch hesitated for only a second before he checked his watch and nodded. "Of course, kiddo. We should still be able to fit in a few more tries before it's time for practice."

After they got their food at the snack bar, they settled in at a shaded open table near Mitch, who was catching up on work emails on his phone.

"So are you excited for your enrichment thing?" Annabelle asked. "That'll be fun to be in Boston and hang out with Samir, huh?"

"Yeah," Jeremy said. "And I'll get to do lots of nerdy math kid stuff."

That's what Mia always called it when Jeremy went off to ninth-grade math class or mathletes. "Have a blast with your nerdy math kid stuff," she'd tease him. "Go . . . equate things!"

"You'll be equating all over the place," Annabelle agreed, keeping her voice jokey, even though she still hated the idea of him being gone for so much of the summer.

He took a big bite of his burger and wiped his mouth with his paper napkin, but a tiny bit of ketchup stuck to the corner.

If Mia were here, she would tease him about the

ketchup and then Annabelle would be the one to tell him where exactly it was so he could get it off. But without Mia here to tease him, Annabelle wasn't quite sure how to tell him it was there.

She waited until he was looking and dabbed at the corner of her own mouth, but he didn't get the hint.

"Looks like Bertha stopped heading north, huh?" she said.

She'd checked the night before, and the shark was back off the coast of Long Island for now.

Jeremy wrinkled his nose, which was a little pink from the morning sun. "Yeah."

"That's probably better, right?" Annabelle said. "Because if she comes back, everyone will get all freaked out again and that'll be bad for your dad's business. And this way the Bluff Point seals are safe."

"Her jaws probably still aren't developed enough to eat a seal," Jeremy said. "And even if she did, that's how sharks survive. It's no worse than you eating that turkey sandwich or me eating a burger."

Annabelle flinched. It wasn't mean, the way Jeremy had said it, but it still felt a little bit like he was a teacher correcting her for getting something wrong.

"You have ketchup on your mouth," she told him, and his cheeks flushed as pink as his nose before he wiped it off.

He readjusted his burger so the meat wasn't about to slide out and took another bite.

"Are you hoping Bertha comes back?" she asked.

Jeremy finished chewing and put his burger down. "Well, my dad has that shark cage thing now, so a diver can go inside to see a shark underwater but stay safe."

Annabelle had heard Mrs. Green complaining to Mom about it. Mr. Green was completely fearless, which meant he had no problem working way up high on the roofs of the tallest houses for his construction job or taking scuba divers to see blue sharks off the coast. Mrs. Green had told Mom she felt all of his fear for him, and it was turning her hair gray.

"But he doesn't take people to see white sharks, right? Only blue ones?"

Blue sharks were big and powerful, too, but nothing close to a great white.

"Right, but some people would probably want to see a white," Jeremy said. "I was thinking he could advertise at the shark museum in Cape Cod. Maybe he could even take scientists, like the ones who tagged her before."

"You think?" Annabelle asked.

Jeremy shrugged. "Also . . . It's probably silly—"

Annabelle cut him off. "I'm sure it's not."

It couldn't be, if Jeremy was thinking it. All of Jeremy's thoughts were smart.

"I was thinking if I showed my dad that I . . ."

But before Jeremy could finish, someone was calling Annabelle's name, and there was Colette at the side of the pool, holding a red and white lane line.

"Hey, Annabelle! Come help me get set up?"

Annabelle looked back at Jeremy, who was flicking his straw with a fingernail.

"Bananabelle!" Mitch whispered, angling his head toward Colette.

"Sorry," Annabelle told Jeremy as she stood up.

She'd been apologizing to Jeremy a lot lately. But he shrugged and pointed to his full carton of mozzarella sticks.

"It's okay," he said. "Go ahead."

Over by the pool, Colette handed Annabelle one end of the first lane line, and Annabelle hooked it in on the near side of the pool while Colette went around to the other side to hook the end she still held. Then Annabelle walked around to take one end of the next line from her.

"Did I ever tell you the story of my first college meet?" Colette asked.

"I know you were an all-American," Annabelle said. Mitch had told her that.

Colette laughed. "Eventually, yeah. But I'm surprised I ever got to race in another meet after my first one."

She handed Annabelle the end of the next line and raised her voice so Annabelle could hear as she carried it back across the pool.

"It was against Stanford. Big rivalry for Berkeley, where I went. I was the biggest recruit. Pressure was on. And you know what I did?"

"What?"

"Lost my balance off the blocks on the 200-meter free and fell right in the water. Talk about a humiliating DQ. I didn't even get to swim my race."

Annabelle was kneeling down to pull the second line straight enough so that she could hook it in, but that made her pause. She'd seen swimmers lose their balance and fall in before, obviously, but it was usually only the least experienced swimmers who did it. Colette had done that when she was a Division I swimmer in *college*?

"At least you didn't swim your whole race as hard as you could and convince yourself you'd actually done great," Annabelle called across the pool. "And somebody else didn't have to swim *her* whole leg even though she knew it wouldn't count."

Colette came back around toward Annabelle, and she didn't bother to bring the third lane line with her.

"You *did* do great," Colette said. "You swam your heart out on that leg, and you kept pace with a girl who's three years older than you and twice your size. There wasn't a single person at that meet who wasn't impressed watching you."

Annabelle pictured the way Kayla and Ruby had stood there, barely cheering for Elisa. And the way they'd all tried to make her feel better after the race because they'd felt sorry for her. They definitely hadn't seemed impressed.

"My swim didn't even count," she pointed out.

Colette shook her head. "Nine times out of ten, that early entry doesn't get called, and maybe we win that relay and you're the hero of the day. Next time you will be. I know it."

And even though Annabelle's timing was all messed up now, there was something about the way Colette said it that made it seem true.

They would race South Shore again in August. If they did well between now and then and beat them next time, the Invitational was still a possibility. Maybe it wasn't realistic to think they could win the medley at that giant tournament, but getting there could be enough for her first year on the team.

Colette clapped her on the shoulder. "Go finish your

lunch, and don't let your dad get you too freaked out about your entry into the water, all right?"

It usually made Annabelle happy when somebody thought Mitch was her dad. She and Mitch looked like they could be related—they both had fair skin and dark blond hair and eyes somewhere between blue and green.

But now, thinking of that unanswered letter buried under her school stuff on her desk, it felt disrespectful to her dad, or something, to let people think Mitch was her father. And unlucky—as if something terrible might happen to him if she pretended he didn't exist.

"Mitch is my stepdad, actually," she said.

"Oh. Sorry," Colette said, even though it wasn't her fault she didn't know.

It would have been easier if Mitch really *was* Annabelle's biological dad. He always showed up when he was supposed to. He made her feel safe and loved and taken care of, like her own dad should have. Like he *had*, at some point. She was sure for a long time he had. But then everything had gotten so messed up.

She hadn't thought about that awful day for ages. But as she walked back to the table where Mitch was finishing another phone call and Jeremy was polishing off his last mozzarella stick, the memory came flooding back.

It was at the end of fourth grade, and her dad was picking her up from practice. She hadn't seen him in a while—he was supposed to see her every Saturday, but sometimes he didn't call and didn't show up. She was excited he was coming that day. She'd perfected her flip turn and she wanted him to see. But then everything was wrong when he showed up.

"Annie!" he shouted, too loud for how close he was. "I've missed you, peanut. How's my girl?"

He was talking funny, as if he had marshmallows inside his cheeks. She'd heard him talk like that a few times before he'd moved out of the house, when she woke up in the middle of the night and found him sitting on the couch with a glass of amber liquid in his hand. But it was scarier now, under the fluorescent lights of the hallway at the Y, than it had been at home in the almost-dark when no one else was there to see. Here, it was impossible to ignore how wrong he sounded, and he was sort of swaying, too.

Annabelle's old coach, Danielle, took him aside and made Annabelle wait outside the locker room long after everyone else had gotten rides home. She sat there on the shiny wooden bench for ages, holding her old purple swim bag in her lap and running her fingers over her initials, which Mom had gotten monogrammed on the top.

She shivered in the air-conditioning and watched the second hand of the clock on the wall. Every time it got close to the twelve at the top, it paused and swung one notch backward before it finished its circle.

Finally, Mom hurried in, squeezed Annabelle tight, then told her to hang on for a minute and rushed into Coach Danielle's office.

Annabelle watched one minute tick by, then two, then three. She heard bits of the conversation that carried past the closed door. Danielle's voice, serious.

"He said he took some kind of new medication."

"A drink or two—not a lot."

"Some kind of interaction with the medicine."

"Not okay to drive."

"Couldn't let him take Annabelle."

Then Mom's voice, too high and tight and squeaky. Thanking Danielle too many times. Apologizing over and over, even though she hadn't done anything wrong.

Annabelle didn't hear Dad's voice, though. He was gone already. He must have slipped out the other door before Mom got there, without even saying goodbye.

And the thing was, she was relieved he was gone, not sad. Relieved she hadn't had to watch him go.

Soon Mom was back, guiding Annabelle to the car, where Mitch waited with Annabelle's favorite music all cued up. And as they drove away, she felt the same kind of warm relief she felt when she was snug in bed while rain poured down outside. Relief that she was here with Mom and Mitch, so she was okay.

After that day, Mom only let Dad see Annabelle if he came over to the house, but he barely ever did. And Annabelle felt that safe-and-warm-at-home-during-a-rainstorm relief every Saturday he didn't show up because, if he was never there, then she didn't have to picture that ashamed look on his face or think about what it meant that he went weeks without calling.

But he was better now. That's what his letter said. And as easy and comfortable as everything would be if Mitch were her biological dad, Mitch *wasn't*, and she had an actual dad who wasn't that far away now. Who wanted to see her, so she should want to see him, too. Shouldn't she?

"Everything okay?" Jeremy asked when she reached the table. He'd finished his food and was reading one of those super-thick fantasy novels he liked so much.

She nodded.

Mitch ended his call. "You ready to get back in the water, Bananabelle?"

For now, she tried to blink away everything except the thought of diving back into the pool.

"Yes," she said, and after three deep breaths, that image of Dad's ashamed face was gone. "Let's do it."

Because she was a swimmer, just like Colette. DQ or no DQ, this was who she was. She could figure out all the more complicated stuff later.

Chapter 11

When it was time for practice, Jeremy took his book over to the shade to read and Mitch went back to the office.

Annabelle joined Elisa and Kayla at the side of the pool. Elisa was only wearing her suit, but Kayla still had on a T-shirt and gym shorts. She usually kept them on until the last second and then left them with her towel instead of in the locker room. If it had been anybody else, somebody might have said something. But everybody knew where Kayla had been last summer, so maybe everybody understood that the bathing suit thing might be hard.

"Hey! I hear you got Jeremy to swim when he wasn't required to," Kayla said, tucking her pin-straight light brown hair behind each ear.

She had the exact same hair as Jeremy, and the same shade of fair white skin and pale brown eyes. Their features were different, but if someone were painting them, they'd use all the same colors. They looked so much alike that when Jeremy had started at the Academy, the older kids had called him "Boy Kayla."

"Well, there were mozzarella sticks involved," Annabelle said, and Kayla laughed.

"That'll do it."

"I'm sure it helped that Annabelle was the one who asked," Elisa said, nudging Annabelle's arm.

Annabelle's cheeks burned, and she glanced over at Jeremy to make sure he hadn't heard that, even though he was too far away and, anyway, he never heard *anything* when he was reading.

Then she changed the subject. "Hey, do you think your mom could drive me to practice tomorrow?" she asked Kayla.

Mitch had reminded her twice that she needed to find a ride, since he and Mom were both busy.

"Aw, I actually have a doctor's appointment, so I'm coming late," Kayla said. "Any other day, though!"

"I could pick you up," Elisa offered, but then she smacked herself in the forehead. "Oops, no I can't. I'm working at the coffee shop and coming straight from there."

And then there was Connor, right behind Annabelle. "I can give you a ride if you need one."

He didn't touch her this time, but all of her skin sizzled, anyway.

Elisa and Kayla exchanged a weird look, but Annabelle didn't have room in her brain to think too much about that or anything else, other than the fact that tomorrow she would be in the same car as Connor Madison. They'd pull up to the pool together. Walk in together. It was almost too amazing to visualize.

At the end of practice, she wrapped herself in her soft purple towel and waved to Mia, who stood over by the snack bar with some other middle school girls. She was about to go over to say hi when Connor called out, "Annabelle! I need your number for tomorrow."

And Mia stared, her mouth partway open, as Connor jogged over to Annabelle and plugged her number into his phone.

"Thanks again," Annabelle said, and Connor grinned. He grinned wider than most people, as if he had more to be happy about.

But then he said, "Cute towel."

Oh no. All the giddiness that had filled her up a moment ago rushed out. She'd forgotten to hide the babyish sea-green monogrammed letters that spelled out her name along one end.

There was Connor, all tall and muscly, looking about twenty years older than she felt, and here she was wrapped in the towel her mom had gotten personalized with her favorite colors, as if she were a six-year-old. She retwisted it so her name was covered, but it was too late.

"Oh. It's from a long time ago," she lied. "Nothing else was clean."

Connor laughed. Because he didn't believe her? Because the towel was so babyish? She wasn't sure. But then he gave her a hand-sizzling high five and said, "See you tomorrow."

He jogged away to meet up with Jordan by the parking lot, and she walked over to Mia, trying to let the sensation of Connor's palm against hers block out any towel-related embarrassment. Mia was too far away to have heard that part, at least.

The other middle school girls had gone into the locker room, so Mia was waiting by herself.

"Good practice?" she asked. Cheerfully. Casually, as if she hadn't seen anything out of the ordinary.

What?

Annabelle was supposed to dissect every detail about the way the random guy at the Creamery said the words

"Enjoy your ice cream," but Mia wasn't going to say *anything* about what had just happened with Connor?

Mia *knew* Annabelle was into Connor, and she'd *watched* him take her phone number. There was no way she didn't realize that was a big deal! But still . . . nothing?

"Practice was great!" Annabelle told her, just as cheerfully and casually.

"Oh good." Mia lowered her voice to a whisper. "I felt so bad after the last meet. That was so terrible with the DQ."

The words were like a giant wave that came out of nowhere and spun Annabelle under, tossing her to the ocean floor. It *had* been terrible, but Annabelle didn't need to hear somebody else come right out and *say* that, especially when she wasn't thinking about it at all.

And okay: Maybe Annabelle shouldn't have left the meet without saying anything to Mia when Mia had stayed to watch her, and maybe she should have included Mia earlier today. But Annabelle knew Mia was only commenting on the DQ now to make herself feel better and Annabelle feel worse.

"Oh, thanks," she said, ordering her voice to stay steady. "But you really don't need to feel bad. Everything's good! Have a fun practice!"

With the other middle *schoolers,* she wanted to add, to rub it in that *Mia* wasn't the one who'd been called up to swim with the high school team. But she stopped herself before she said it.

As Mia went into the locker room, Annabelle's phone buzzed with a text, so she pulled it out of her bag.

It's Connor. Hey there.

That's all Connor had said, but while Annabelle waited for Mitch to pick her up, she drained the battery on her phone reading those four words over and over.

It was like Mitch always said: She couldn't control how other people acted, but she could control how it affected her. And she wasn't going to let Mia's fake-sympathetic words bring her down. Not today.

The next morning, Mom kissed Annabelle's cheek on her way out the door to work.

"Tutoring at—"

"Eleven," Annabelle finished for her. "And Janine's money is on the kitchen table. I know. And when I wait for you to get me after practice, I'm supposed to read the next chapter of the summer reading book and then review Spanish note cards."

Mom smiled. "I'm proud of you. For going for what you want with the high school team and keeping up with everything else."

Annabelle let Mom kiss her cheek on the way out and mumbled "Thanks." But it still seemed like she hadn't done anything *that* impressive for Mom to be proud of. Like maybe Mom's expectations were sort of low.

After Mom was gone, she pulled out the letter from her dad. She read it again even though she knew it by heart, and she tried to imagine whether her dad looked different now and where he'd been sitting and what he'd been thinking as he wrote it.

What would Mom say if she knew he'd written? Back after Dad had first moved out, Mom had acted like it was a huge priority for Annabelle to see him.

"Your time with your father is important," she'd say, making Annabelle turn down invitations to friends' houses on "Dad days." One time she'd said no when Mitch invited them to go away for the weekend with him and his daughters.

"Annabelle needs to have a relationship with her dad," she'd told him. "I can't be the reason that doesn't happen."

But then after that awful swim practice, Mom had stopped objecting when things came up on Saturdays.

She'd decided it was fine to move all the way to Gray Island, even. That was after Dad had stopped calling completely, but still.

Would she want Annabelle to have a relationship with her dad now, or did she think it was too late?

Would she believe that Dad was really better? Or would she make a big thing of only letting Annabelle see him if he came to Gray Island and she and Mitch supervised?

Dad's letter was the biggest thing Annabelle had ever kept from her mom. But she wanted to figure it out *herself*—how she felt about it and what she wanted to do. She didn't want Mom's opinions drowning out her own.

She was reading Dad's words one last time when a text came in from Mia.

Saw Mr. Derrickson at the Bagelry and he and my dad talked for ages about some new whaling exhibit in Boston. My dad thinks he's "such a great guy." Little does he know!!!

And for the first time in ages, a text from Mia made Annabelle smile for real.

Yeah well he doesn't have to take Mr. Derrickson's tests!! she wrote back, and Mia's next text came immediately.

Ugh I wish I could force him to as punishment for leaving AGAIN. He's going to NYC today. He's like never here anymore.

Annabelle sent back an **ugh I'm sorry** and checked the time.

She really had to leave for tutoring, but she really wished she could call Mia.

Mia had complained before about how much her dad traveled but not for a long time. This last text felt like the most honest thing either of them had told the other all summer, and Annabelle wanted to capitalize on it. Letting it go felt like wasting a strong start to a race with lazy first strokes.

She thought maybe she could even talk to Mia about *her* dad if she called her right now. She didn't like talking about him, so she usually used Mom's "He's not in the picture" line. Mia had pushed it one time and asked why not, and Annabelle had said the other thing Mom sometimes told people: that he "had some things to work out before he could be in her life."

But maybe she could tell Mia the rest. Mia didn't know her dad, so she wouldn't get upset or protective like Mom. Maybe Mia could help her figure out whether she wanted to write back or not, and what she wanted to say if she did.

Or maybe Mia would be so busy getting texts from Reagan that she'd barely pay attention and she'd give Annabelle some too-fast, too-definite response. Like "Of course you should see him, he's your dad." Or, "Isn't your life fine without him? Why would you want to risk messing everything up?" Or, "Why don't you just ask your mom?"

Annabelle sighed. Whether she wanted to talk to Mia right now or not, she couldn't keep Janine waiting. She'd promised Mom she'd be on time. So she sent Mia a string of hearts and then dropped her things into the basket of her bike and started off toward the library.

But a few minutes into her ride, her phone buzzed with another text, and this one was from Connor.

Hey HB.

Below that, three dots showed her that he was typing.

She pulled to the side of the path to wait for his next message.

We're getting a ride with Jordan & eating at the pool. Be at your place in 15?

Fifteen.

Fifteen minutes? That's when her tutoring session started. It would take her almost that long to ride back home and get her things for practice.

She swatted away a bug that buzzed close to her cheek, but as soon as it flew away, another one buzzed over.

It was too late to cancel tutoring. Janine would have left already to meet her at the library. And Mom would completely freak out if she didn't go.

But what could she do? Tell Connor she couldn't leave that early and then have to miss practice, when she needed every chance she had to prove herself before the next meet? Give up the chance to ride to the pool with him? Tell him the reason she couldn't—that she wasn't smart enough to pass eighth grade by herself next year, so she needed someone helping her all summer?

Janine would still get paid since it was too late for a cancellation, so she probably wouldn't mind that much. And Annabelle would think of a way to make it okay with Mom. She'd do extra work all weekend or something.

She sent Janine an apology text and texted Connor a quick **sounds good** before pedaling home as fast as she could. She didn't have any choice, she told herself.

Chapter 12

Annabelle had barely finished shoving all her stuff into her swim bag when a blue minivan pulled up in front of her house. The girl who was driving had long, highlighted hair and olive skin kind of like Mia's, and Jordan sat in the passenger seat with a blue baseball cap pulled low. The back door slid open.

"Hummingbird!" Connor said. "This is Natalie, Jordan's sister."

Connor wore a dark green Gray Island High lacrosse T-shirt that made his eyes even greener than usual. He pulled his swim bag toward him so there would be plenty of room for Annabelle, even though it wouldn't have been in her way, and her breath caught at the chivalrous gesture.

Of course, then he and Jordan spent most of the drive talking about some Red Sox trade that might happen while she just sat there. But eventually he turned to her and said, "You like baseball?"

Annabelle felt the way she did at school when a teacher called on her and she wasn't expecting it. She wanted to think of something interesting to say, something *right*, but words tangled in her brain.

Finally she shrugged. "It's okay."

The truth was, she'd loved to watch baseball with her dad when she was younger. But her dad was a Yankees fan, so she'd been one, too. And she knew better than to admit that in Red Sox territory.

She and Dad had gone to Yankees games every once in a while. One time when they drove to the stadium in the Bronx, there was so much traffic that they missed the first three innings. As they sat there in the car, inching forward and listening to the game on the radio, she gnawed on her bottom lip until her teeth cut through the skin, afraid her dad would be upset about being so late. But it was a good day, so he cheered and high-fived Annabelle when one of the Yankees hit a home run, and they listed all the foods they were going to buy when they got to the stadium: hot dogs and ice cream and soft pretzels and popcorn. And then he really did buy all of that when they finally arrived. They could barely carry it all to their seats.

They'd been supposed to go again at the end of fourth grade, for her tenth birthday. Dad had said that was her present, to go to a game and bring any friend she wanted. So she'd told her old New Jersey best friend, Gabriela, because Gabi was the biggest Yankees fan she knew.

But then after that awful swim practice, Mom didn't want him driving her anymore. He never brought up the game again, and Annabelle was more relieved than disappointed because it would have been horrible to listen to her own father admit that he couldn't take her to the game because Mom wouldn't allow it after how badly he'd messed up. To see him shrink down like a kid getting yelled at by a teacher. It was better to forget about the whole plan and hope Gabi would forget, too.

When Natalie pulled up to the curb in front of the pool, Jordan said goodbye and closed the door, but Connor said, "Thanks for the ride, Nat! Hope you're not too bored without us the rest of the day!" And then he gave Natalie the same silly salute he'd given Annabelle, Kayla, and Elisa the other day.

"I *think* I'll manage," Natalie said, and Connor laughed, even though nothing was that funny. But it was nice that Connor had made a special effort to say thank you.

Mia's cousin with the serious boyfriend had said that it's good if the person you like is sweet to *you*, but it's even better if they're nice to everybody else, too, even when they don't have to be. That's how you know it's in their true nature and they're not just trying to impress you.

Annabelle wasn't positive if Connor was trying to impress her, but he was definitely nice to everybody. As they walked up to the gate, he greeted the sign-in guy, Doug, and asked if Doug had seen the Sox game last night and what he thought of the trade rumors.

The pool was packed with moms and little kids wearing swimmies, plus a few older people swimming laps. Annabelle could hear Mitch inside her head, saying those swimmies caused more problems than they fixed because kids who wore them didn't learn to swim for real, and then what happened if they ever jumped in the pool when their parents weren't looking?

Mitch had said that in front of his daughters when they were visiting last summer, and they'd rolled their eyes. "*We* used to wear swimmies," they'd reminded him. "You might not have approved, but you weren't the one there watching us."

Annabelle loved Mitch's daughters, who included her in everything they did when they came to the island

and talked to her about what was going on in their lives as if she were old enough to understand. But she didn't always like the way they treated Mitch. They got annoyed when he gave them advice about capitalizing on opportunities and visualizing their success, and sometimes they made comments like that, about him not being around for stuff when they were younger.

But this was *Mitch*, who scheduled his meetings around Annabelle's swim meets and called his daughters every Sunday and invited them to visit over every school break. Mitch was nothing like Annabelle's dad, who had just disappeared.

Well, until the letter arrived, anyway.

Jordan went straight for the snack bar and Connor trailed a few steps behind him, but Annabelle stopped inside the gate. Connor had said they were eating at the pool—but did that mean all of them together? Was he expecting her to hang out with him and Jordan until practice? Or did he figure he'd done his job and now she was on her own?

But Connor came back to where she was standing and flicked the bottom of her ponytail. She knew the ends of her hair didn't have any nerve endings, but it still felt like they tingled.

"You hungry?" he asked.

She smiled the closed-mouth, school-picture smile she used to practice with Mia and nodded. That was about all she could manage, standing this close to Connor. So close that he could easily reach out and flick her hair again, or touch her arm or her shoulder.

Together, they headed to the snack bar, and Annabelle wondered what those moms with little kids wearing swimmies were thinking—whether they assumed she and Connor were a couple, and what it would feel like to slide her fingers through his if they actually were.

Connor high-fived the pretty college-aged lifeguard as they passed, and then he high-fived Ruby, who was outside the snack bar talking to Jordan. Her reddish-brown hair was twisted up into a clip, and pink bikini straps peeked out from the top of a tissue-thin T-shirt with some kind of band logo on it. She must have had a racing suit for practice in the locker room. Annabelle's black suit didn't feel quite so special anymore, in comparison.

"Fiiiiinally," Ruby said. "You're here."

Jordan pushed the door open for himself and then Connor swooped in to hold it for Ruby and Annabelle.

"Great shirt, Rubes!" he said. "Love their music!"

And he stood next to *Ruby*, not Annabelle, as they waited to order. Ruby went on and on about some concert she'd gone to, and Connor focused all his attention on her. Annabelle felt the same way she had when he'd commented on her monogrammed towel. Like he was so, so much older than she was and she didn't belong here with him at all.

Once they'd ordered, Ruby took her Caesar salad to a table in the shade, and Connor and Jordan followed with their burgers. Annabelle waited and waited for her grilled cheese, which was taking forever. By the time she got to the table, Ruby was laughing so hard she made a big show of barely being able to breathe.

"Okay, okay, me next. Coach Colette or that girl Paige?" she asked.

"Colette," Jordan said right away, but Connor glanced over at Annabelle.

"Oh, sorry!" Ruby said. "Should we stop? Don't want to corrupt the youth!"

"It's fine," Annabelle said. She tore the crust off one side of her grilled cheese and then winced when it burned her fingertips.

She wanted to say something else, too, to prove she wasn't so babyish that they had to worry about corrupting her. Except she wasn't completely sure what they were doing.

Connor drummed his fingers against the edge of the table. "Yeah. I guess Colette."

"You *guess*?" Jordan said. "It's *Colette*!" He sighed in disbelief. "She's amazing."

"Sorry to break it to you, but I don't think you're her type," Ruby teased, poking Jordan's arm with her plastic fork.

"Yeah, yeah. I saw her girlfriend waiting for her in the parking lot after practice yesterday, too," Jordan said. "Doesn't mean I can't admire her from afar. Or from up close. Anywhere, really. I'm not particular."

Annabelle was glad Connor just took a bite of his burger instead of gushing about how gorgeous and incredible Colette was.

Ruby turned to Annabelle, and the smile on her face was way too sweet. Cotton-candy-sticking-to-her-lips-and-turning-the-corners-of-her-mouth-blue sweet. "The game is who you'd rather, like . . . spend an afternoon alone with."

"I understand the game," Annabelle said.

Jordan hooted with laughter, making Annabelle drop the piece of grilled cheese crust she'd been holding.

"Yeah. Who you'd rather spend an afternoon *aloooone* with." He wiggled his eyebrows so many times Annabelle thought they might wiggle right off his face. "All right, my turn. Abby Goldberg or Emily Aarons?"

Annabelle had never heard of them, so they must have been from Gray Island High.

Connor made a face. "Emily, I guess."

"Seriously?" Jordan asked. "What, you want to help her tune that trombone?"

This time Connor was the one who erupted in laughter, and Annabelle's stomach turned. Ruby laughed, too, even though there was no way she knew Emily, since she was a summer person. Then she went again, even though she'd just taken a turn.

"Okay, Annabelle. I have one for you. What's Kayla's little brother's name? Jesse?"

All three of them looked at Annabelle.

"Jeremy, right?" Connor said.

"Jer-e-my!" Jordan sang. "Somebody's blushing!"

"No, I'm not!" Annabelle said.

Which was silly. She *was* blushing—she could feel how warm her cheeks were. But it wasn't because they'd mentioned Jeremy, exactly. It was the intensity of all three of them looking at her at once and the whole idea of her and Jeremy . . . like that.

"I was going to say Jeremy or that funny kid, Scotty Gorman," Ruby said. "But I think we have our answer."

Annabelle shook her head. "Jeremy's one of my best friends. It's not like that."

Connor reached across the table and put his hand on Annabelle's arm for a second. "Leave HB alone."

But Ruby kept going. "You and little Green would be adorable!"

Adorable.

She sounded like she was talking about babies or puppies. Like she had to remind Connor and Jordan that Annabelle was so much younger than the rest of them.

"I wouldn't choose either of them," Annabelle said, but then she pictured Jeremy's just-out-of-the-pool spiky hair and the ketchup in the corner of his mouth the other day, and she felt awful. "I mean, not for . . . uh . . ."

Jordan squawked out a laugh that sounded like a seagull's cry. "*Aloooone* time? Why not?"

Annabelle had to change the subject. She hadn't wanted Connor and them to ignore her, but this kind of attention was all wrong, like an icy blast of air-conditioning instead of a nice, calm breeze.

"My turn! I'll go next!" she said.

And now she had to come up with something good. Something that would convince them she wasn't just some innocent little kid. *Come on, think!*

"What, are you going through the whole alphabetical roster in your head?" Jordan asked.

The two girls had to be equally matched in some way, she got that. Jeremy and Scotty both had close to the same color hair and were around the same height. Coach Colette and Paige, too. Maybe two of the girls on the freestyle relay team? Then she had it.

"Coach Katherine or Elisa."

Katherine was the old high school coach who left after last summer. She and Elisa both had freckles, bright blue eyes, broad shoulders, and muscular legs.

"Good one!" Connor said. But then Jordan chimed in.

"The manly girls!" he said in an extra-deep voice.

"No!" Annabelle said. "That's not . . . I didn't mean . . ."

"You guys." Ruby shook her head, but she was smiling. Smiling, even though Elisa was her friend!

Connor and Jordan both picked Elisa, but Annabelle's heart lurched.

It wasn't hard to make guys laugh if you acted sort of mean—either about them or about someone else. But she didn't want to be the kind of girl who had to be mean to make guys like her. And she definitely didn't want to be mean about Elisa.

Before she could think of any way to fix things, Jordan puffed his chest out, and in an extra-deep voice he said, "All right, ladies. Me or Madison?"

Ruby threw a piece of lettuce across the table at him. It stuck to his gray T-shirt and left a Parmesan-cheese-flecked wet spot when he flicked it off.

"Hey!" He threw one fry that hit the front of Ruby's shirt, and then a second fry, which bounced off her shoulder and hit Annabelle.

"Geez," Connor said. "Maybe Hummingbird and I need to move to another table."

He looked at Annabelle, his green eyes open a little extra wide and his mouth twitching at the corners. Expecting her to join in the joking.

Ruby would have come up with a funny, flirtatious reply. Mia, too. But Annabelle's mind went as fuzzy as it did when she was taking one of Mr. Derrickson's history tests.

Her phone buzzed with one text and then another, and she reached for it.

"Is it Jeremy?" Ruby teased, which set Jordan off into another round of shouting, "Jer-e-my!"

But it was Mom. Of course.

Chapter 13

Until Annabelle saw Mom's name on the screen of her phone, she'd managed to keep her guilt about skipping tutoring at the edges of her mind. Like gray clouds in the distance, threatening a rainstorm far enough away that it wasn't time to go inside yet. But now those gray clouds were ready to open up right over her head.

Where are you? the first text said.

And then: **I just heard from Janine.**

There was a missed call from Mom, too, which she hadn't heard because the pool had bad reception.

Another text then. **I need you to respond! I'm worried.**

"I'll be right back," Annabelle croaked.

The texts and calls weren't going to stop if she didn't reply. But that word *worried* dug its way under her skin and made her want to scream.

Angry, okay. It would make sense for Mom to be angry, since she cared more about Annabelle's tutoring than any swim practice or race result. But Annabelle had *told* Janine why she couldn't go to tutoring, and she was sure Janine would have told Mom.

What did Mom think was going to happen to her if she got to the pool a little early? Did Mom think she'd get a blistering sunburn because she'd be too irresponsible to reapply sunscreen? That she'd guzzle caffeinated soda instead of water and end up dehydrated?

Did Mom think her chances of doing decently in eighth grade were so tiny that one missed tutoring session would doom her?

Whenever Mom said she was worried, Annabelle couldn't help thinking of her dad. The hushed conversations she'd overheard at night back at the New Jersey house: "I'm worried about the drinking. I'm worried you haven't started looking for another job. I'm worried you don't seem like your old self."

I'm fine, Annabelle texted back. **My ride came early. I'll pay for the tutoring myself.**

It took a while for Mom's reply to come through.

If I didn't have a lunch meeting, I'd come get you right now. We'll be having a serious conversation this afternoon.

Annabelle sighed. **OK**, she texted back.

She tried to push down the dread of that "serious conversation" as she shoved her cell phone to the bottom of her bag. She wasn't going to let it sabotage her practice or her time with Connor.

When she got back to the table, she made herself focus all of her attention on him. His ears, which were no longer sunburned at the tips. The extra-blond strands in the front of his hair. Those peridot-green eyes. The string that had come loose at the bottom of his T-shirt sleeve.

They were still playing the game, and Jordan tried to get Annabelle and Ruby to choose between Billy, the friendly pool janitor who was probably in his fifties, and Doug at the front desk, whose shirt was damp with sweat even on the cool days but who knew every single swimmer's name and always said hi.

For once, a reply jumped into Annabelle's brain.

"I don't know," she said to Jordan. "Why don't you choose first?"

She felt bad afterward, even though everyone laughed. Lily Ericson-Bentley, who was in Annabelle's class at the Academy, would probably point out that the only reason they laughed was because they were uncomfortable with homosexuality on some level, and that was wrong. Lily would have a problem with pretty much every part of this game, and she'd be brave enough to tell Jordan and Connor and Ruby exactly why.

Pretty soon, everyone tired of the game and Annabelle relaxed a little. Ruby asked Jordan about some sort-of-famous person whose lawn he mowed—Dennis Martin, who directed movies, apparently. She made a big fuss out of how great the movies were, and Annabelle nodded along, even though she hadn't heard of any of them.

"He's a good guy, actually," Jordan said.

"What?" Connor said. "I thought you'd never even spoken to him."

"Well, not directly," Jordan admitted. "His wife is the one who sets everything up with the lawn mowing. But I heard him on the phone the other day while he was sitting out by the pool. You could tell it was a business call, but he was real laid-back about it."

Connor grinned and patted Jordan on the back. "Right. Yeah, I'm sure it's only a matter of time before you turn on the old Bernstein charm and Dennis Martin's inviting you over to hang out by the pool and tell him all your great ideas about his next movie."

Ruby took her hair out of its clip. "That pool is *ridiculous*."

"You swam in it?" Annabelle asked.

"Um, no." She shook her head so that her hair swished against her shoulders and the flowery smell of her shampoo overtook the usual pool smells of grease and chlorine and sunscreen. "Dennis Martin's pool. I wish."

"Someday, Rubes," Jordan said, "I *will* charm Dennis Martin, just you wait and see. And then you and I will be floating around in his pool and he'll be asking us to do a cameo in his new movie."

Connor caught Annabelle's eye and raised one eyebrow before turning to Jordan. "Good luck with that, man," he said. Then he pointed over to the grassy lawn where the game of cornhole was always set up: two slanted wooden boards with holes on the back end, about ten feet apart, and little bean bags you tried to throw onto the boards or into the holes at the back. "Wanna play cornhole?"

Annabelle used to play all the time with Mia and Jeremy, but Connor was asking Jordan, not her, and she couldn't get up the nerve to invite herself to join.

So she slipped out of the shorts and T-shirt she'd worn over her suit, slathered on some more sunscreen, and settled on a chair with her summer reading book. If she could get through a whole chapter and explain it to Mom on the way home, even though she'd missed tutoring, Mom might not be *quite* as mad.

Ruby spread out on the lawn chair next to her with a magazine and actually sounded interested when she asked what Annabelle was reading. "Oh, I love that book!" she said.

But with Ruby right next to her, Annabelle was too embarrassed to hold her index card under each line and move it down the page to keep her eyes focused. And it was too hard to pay attention to tiny black words crammed too close together on a page when Connor Madison was nearby, chatting with the pretty college-aged lifeguard as Jordan divided up the beanbags and waited for him.

Connor finally joined Jordan, and they started their game. But now Annabelle was too thirsty to read, so she walked over to the water fountain. And when she peeked back at Connor and Jordan, Connor was watching her, too.

She gave him that closed-mouth smile she'd practiced in the mirror with Mia, but it widened into a grin when she heard Jordan yell at him.

"It's your turn, Mads! Come on!"

She'd made Connor Madison forget it was his turn. She'd never felt so powerful in her life.

Chapter 14

Mom was there at the end of practice, standing so close to the edge of the pool that her beige linen work dress was dotted with water spots. When she pushed her sunglasses up to the top of her head, there was that worry line, creasing the triangle of skin between her eyebrows and her nose.

And there was Mia, standing in the middle of a group of girls, watching Annabelle's mom with her whole body angled forward to listen instead of paying attention to what the other girls were saying.

"Get your things and let's go," Mom said. "Now, please, Annabelle."

Mia caught Annabelle's eye and frowned, as if to say she was sorry Annabelle was so obviously in trouble. It was the same frown she gave Annabelle when teachers asked to talk to her after class, and it made her want to scream. At least Connor was busy talking to Jordan and the other guys instead of watching her get scolded by her mother as if she were a six-year-old who'd gotten caught sneaking an extra cookie.

She caught up with Elisa on the way to the locker room.

"So do you work at Beach Buzz?" she asked. That was the most popular coffee shop in town, on the cobblestoned Main Street across from the preppy shops that only summer people shopped at. They always hired lots of extra high school kids for the summer.

"Yeah, I just started," Elisa said.

"Lots of fancy summer people asking for all those fancy drinks?" Annabelle asked.

"So many fancy drinks!" Elisa said. "I guarantee you they sell, like, two half-caf skinny iced mocha-caramel-whatever lattes the whole rest of the year and then two thousand in the summer."

Annabelle was relieved to reassure herself that things were normal with Elisa, to sort of . . . counteract what had happened during the game, when Jordan had called Elisa manly and laughed. But it struck her how easy it was to bond with girls, too, by sort of making fun of someone else. When in doubt, say something mildly insulting about summer people to another year-round islander. Or at school, complain about a teacher. Or for the kids who went to the public school, complain about kids who went to the Academy. She didn't like it when she was part of the group that got complained about, but here she was doing it, too.

Then her wet ponytail thwacked against her right ear and a tan hand grazed Elisa's shoulder.

"What's up, Pricey? Fun hanging out with you, Hummingbird!" Connor called on his way into the guys' locker room.

Elisa raised her eyebrows, and Annabelle wanted so much to talk to her about Connor. To get Elisa to help her analyze all of the interactions she'd had with him today the way she knew Mia probably wouldn't.

But Mom was waiting and only getting angrier, so she hurried to get dressed and then hurried to the car, where tulle and fake flowers from one of Mom's parties littered the passenger-seat floor.

"You're going to call Janine to apologize as soon as we get home," Mom said as she started the engine. "And you'll be on dishwashing and trash and laundry-folding duty until I say otherwise. What were you *thinking*?"

She didn't wait for Annabelle to answer, though. She kept on talking, and Annabelle zoned out enough that she only caught a few select words. *Irresponsible.* *Inconsiderate.* And, of course, *worried.*

Annabelle looked out the window as they left the pool. She watched five or six kids chasing each other around the emerald-green lawn of a summer house. They were about ten or eleven—around the age Annabelle had been when she'd moved to the island. Even though the car windows were closed, their shouts and squeals streamed in.

"And from now on," Mom said, "if I don't approve of your ride to practice, you don't go. Got it?"

Annabelle nodded, but it was hard to care too much about her punishment after Colette had put her with the second-fastest freestyle relay team during practice and Connor had gone out of his way to flick her ponytail twice.

"You get one warning here, Belle," Mom added. "This is it. If anything like this happens again, you're showing me you can't handle the extra responsibility of the high school team, and it's back to the middle school team for good."

That got Annabelle's attention. "I won't mess up again," she promised.

Because she couldn't lose being on the high school team.

Because after today, it didn't seem all that impossible that a guy like Connor really *might* choose a girl like her. And that would be as good as—or maybe even better than—an A in Mr. Derrickson's history class.

"Oh," Mom added as she pulled into their driveway. "Mrs. Sloane called this morning. Something opened up in her schedule tomorrow afternoon, so she wants to meet us then."

Annabelle's throat went dry. She was supposed to have so much time left before the meeting. And it was supposed to be in the morning, not in the afternoon when she had practice.

"It's good, I figure," Mom said. "The sooner the better."

"I'll miss practice," Annabelle pointed out.

But she could have recited her mom's response along with her. "School comes first." Always.

Chapter 15

It was strange to be back at school during the summer. In the hallways of the middle school building, the maroon lockers sat open and empty, and the bulletin boards were stripped bare. It turned out those bulletin boards were covered in peeling gray-blue paint under the bright paper teachers usually covered them with and speckled with old thumbtack holes and the occasional shine of a staple that hadn't been pulled out. No "exemplary student work" hanging on them now.

Annabelle followed her mom to Mrs. Sloane's office, and they sat on the benches in the hall where kids had to wait for their punishments when they'd gotten in trouble.

She thought back to the first time she'd been inside Mrs. Sloane's office, when she visited the Academy the summer before sixth grade. Back then, she still let Mom choose her outfits and braid her hair to the side on special days. She'd worn a pale yellow dress and ballet flats that had a shimmer in the leather, and she'd tried to count the shimmery flecks as she waited for Mrs. Sloane to let her in.

She'd known the answers to all the questions Mom had made her practice answering: her favorite subject, and what she did outside of school, and her favorite book.

But then Mrs. Sloane didn't ask any of those things. She spent most of the time peering down through her glasses at Annabelle's fifth-grade report card and the results of the tests Annabelle had taken as part of her application to the Academy. The only thing she asked was how hard Annabelle was willing to work.

"Really hard," Annabelle had promised.

Now, looking at her final seventh-grade report card, Mrs. Sloane would probably think she'd lied.

The office door swung open, and its creak echoed in the empty hallway.

"I'm so glad it worked out for you to come in today," Mrs. Sloane said, shaking Mom's hand first and then Annabelle's.

"Thank you so much for making the time to meet with us," Mom babbled. "Nothing is a bigger priority to us than Annabelle's schoolwork, and we think it's so important to talk about this year now, while we have time to make some changes before eighth grade starts."

Mom took a seat at one end of the hard, gray sofa that sat against the wall of Mrs. Sloane's office, a few feet away from her cluttered desk, and pulled out Annabelle's learning plan. An educational psychologist had written it up after Annabelle had all that extra testing in the winter of sixth grade, just a few months into her first year at the Academy, when she was already falling behind. Mrs. Sloane walked over to her desk chair, and Mom talked and talked about accommodations and tutoring and final exams.

Annabelle sat down on the other end of the couch and examined the gray and white area rug underneath her feet. The rug hadn't been there the last time she was here, and she tried to imagine Mrs. Sloane picking it out.

Mrs. Sloane had probably wanted something that wasn't too cheerful, since almost nobody went into her office for a happy conversation. Something too cheerful would rub that in.

"Annabelle?"

Mrs. Sloane's voice now. So Mom had finally stopped talking.

"I'm sorry," Annabelle said. "What was the question?"

Mrs. Sloane gave her a patient smile, but it was the kind of patient that strained to cover up exasperation. Annabelle was an expert on that kind of patient, because she got that same look from teachers. The nicer ones, anyway, who bothered to hide their annoyance.

"It wasn't a question," Mrs. Sloane said. "More of an observation. That the end of the year proved challenging for you."

That was a school word, *challenging*.

Last year, Annabelle's English teacher had made the class brainstorm transition words they could use in their essays—*however* and *as a result* and *in addition*. Annabelle imagined a classroom full of teachers brainstorming words they could use to keep the kids who weren't smart from feeling too bad. *Challenge* was the big winner. The comments on her report cards were always peppered with different forms of that word. *Challenge, challenging, challenges*. And then there was the old classic: *developing*.

Boys had looked at her differently ever since her *body* had started to "develop." That's the way Mia's mom had put it, when they'd gone on that shopping trip and Annabelle had come out of the dressing room wearing that striped shirt. That something that clingy was going to draw a lot of attention since she was so "developed." When it came to her body, Annabelle was ahead of Mia and almost everybody else. When it came to school, she was always stuck "developing"— her reading skills, her understanding of essay writing, her ability to conjugate Spanish verbs—and never quickly enough.

"What do you think we should do?" Mom asked Mrs. Sloane.

"Well, there are a few things Ms. Ames suggested," Mrs. Sloane started. "For one thing, there's summer work."

Mrs. Sloane was wearing a necklace with a thick silver chain and a stone in the front. It looked like the pink quartz rocks that were buried in the sand all over Gray Island, except it was bigger than any stone Annabelle had ever found, and it was a perfect oval.

Mom was off again, listing all the work Annabelle was doing with Janine, as if that might earn Annabelle bonus points for next year. Or earn *Mom* bonus points for doing so much to help. Make it clear that it wasn't because of *her* that Annabelle had so much trouble.

Mom had never had this kind of trouble in school. She'd gone to a great college, gotten a great marketing job in New York City right after she finished. It was Dad who hadn't even made it through his sophomore year at his much-less-impressive college.

Mrs. Sloane nodded, and Annabelle focused on the way the iridescent flecks and swirls in the stone on her necklace caught the light. She was almost certain it *was* pink quartz, which the waves and sand wore down into smooth, roundish pebbles. She couldn't understand how it was so big and smooth, though.

"That's a great start, certainly," Mrs. Sloane said. "It's important for Annabelle to have supports in place to keep up with the required work. But Ms. Ames and I think we're at a point where we need to step back and address some of the underlying issues that are leading to Annabelle's difficulties."

Difficulties. Another word Annabelle heard a lot of. Not quite as gentle as *challenges*, so teachers only pulled it out when they really wanted to make a point.

Mrs. Sloane kept going: about test scores and Annabelle's processing speed and working memory.

Then she leaned back, and the shiny pink stone bounced once against her rib cage before settling on top of her blouse. Mom was scribbling in her notebook, nodding as she wrote. The worry line between her eyebrows stretched down all the way to the bridge of her nose.

Annabelle wanted to grab Mom's pen and snap it in half so the ink would leak all over that not-overly-cheerful gray and white rug.

Mrs. Sloane picked up a marked-up copy of Annabelle's fourth-quarter report card with the C in Spanish circled in blue.

"We could consult with the educational psychologist who did Annabelle's testing. At the time, he didn't recommend a Spanish waiver, but based on Annabelle's recent report card, it wouldn't be unusual for her to be excused from a foreign language."

"Wait. You want to kick me out of Spanish?" Annabelle asked.

She actually liked Spanish, even though it was hard. They sang songs to remember new words and watched videos to learn about Spanish culture, and Señora Melkoff once said that learning Spanish had been hard for her, too, but then everything had clicked when she spent a summer in Chile in high school. Annabelle thought things might still click for her, too.

"No one's kicking you out of anything," Mrs. Sloane said. "But your particular learning profile means that the skills you need to master a foreign language are still . . ."

"Developing?" Annabelle suggested.

"Exactly," Mrs. Sloane agreed. "Ms. Ames wouldn't be free every language period to meet with you, but sometimes you'd be able to work together during that time, and on other days you would have your own individual study hall. You could do your homework right on the bench outside my office, and I could keep an eye on you."

On the bad-kid bench? Where every single person in the seventh and eighth grades could see her?

Mom was nodding. "It does sound like that could take some of the pressure off." She turned to Annabelle. "You could get your math and science homework done during that free period sometimes, and then you'd have more time for history and English at night."

Mrs. Sloane set down the report card, took off the glasses she'd had perched halfway down her nose, and folded them up. "Annabelle, do you think you could give your mom and me a moment?"

Annabelle's throat went dry. Was this when Mrs. Sloane was going to say it? That the "qualified day student" financial aid wasn't for students who could only get Cs? That maybe Annabelle didn't belong at the Academy at all?

She nodded and walked out into the hallway, where she sat down on the bench and stared at those bare bulletin boards. For the first time in ages, she thought of the room that was supposed to be hers at Dad's old apartment in New Jersey.

The room had a twin bed with a white wicker frame, but Dad had never gotten sheets or a comforter, so the shiny blue mattress had stayed bare. The bed had belonged to his friend's daughter, and so had the other things he'd gotten for the room: an empty dresser and a little white desk with a lavender-painted bulletin board hanging on the wall. She'd forgotten about the bulletin board until this very moment.

It was so heartbreakingly optimistic of her dad to put a bulletin board in the room where Annabelle was supposed to be able to stay on weekends but never actually did. As if she'd be there enough to want to tack up mementos and reminders.

Or maybe the bulletin board was a random hand-me-down he took from his friend without thinking about it at all.

Except, no. It hadn't been the only thing on the wall, she remembered now. There was also a poster of her favorite swimmer, Katie Ledecky, and Dad must have picked that out just for her. Even though he hadn't decorated the rest of that crummy, too-white apartment, even when things were bad, he'd chosen a poster for her wall and gotten furniture for her room.

He *had* really cared, even when it didn't seem like it.

Maybe he'd kept that stuff all this time and brought it to his new place in Boston, hoping someday she'd stay there and stick stuff on the bulletin board and give him a reason to put sheets on the bed.

The door to Mrs. Sloane's office swung open and Mom came out.

"Come on, Belle," she said. "Let's go."

She didn't make Annabelle thank Mrs. Sloane for her time. She didn't tell Annabelle to stop biting her bottom lip, even though Annabelle could tell by the sting that she'd chewed the front part raw. She rushed past so fast that Annabelle could feel an extra breeze on top of the air-conditioning, and she didn't say a word until they made it outside and the real, barely salty breeze hit them.

"Well!" Her voice came out too loud, as if she were wearing earbuds and couldn't hear herself. "That gives us a lot to talk about. Don't you think?"

"What did she say to you?" Annabelle asked. "Is she . . . did she say anything about my financial aid?"

"That's not something you need to think about, Belle."

Mom said it in the same definite, no-nonsense voice she used on the phone with her event-planning clients.

Absolutely, the party will be perfect even if it rains. I know you'll love the blue hyacinths even though you wanted pink.

As if just by telling Annabelle she shouldn't think about the financial aid, Annabelle would stop.

As they headed back toward town, Mia texted to ask where Annabelle was and if everything was okay. It was four, which meant the high school practice was ending and the middle school one was about to start.

Annabelle didn't want to say anything that would give Mia a reason to frown her sympathy frown again, so she put her phone away without replying.

They drove past a brand-new house—even bigger than the other ones in the neighborhood and new-cedar brown all over. Somebody had torn an old house down and started over instead of adding on to what had been there. She wasn't sure what would bother her mom more: a house that clashed so completely with everything else on the street like this one did, or a house that clashed with itself—part new and part old—like theirs used to.

And she couldn't help thinking how hard it must be for Mom to have a daughter who didn't match. To sit there inside Mrs. Sloane's office, probably wishing she had married someone as smart as Mitch the first time around, so her kid could be as successful as she was.

Chapter 16

There was a meet on Friday afternoon, so at least Annabelle had a chance to redeem herself after the last one. It was against a team from the mainland—one they hadn't raced before, so nobody really knew what to expect.

When it was time for the medley relay, Elisa gathered Kayla, Ruby, and Annabelle together for a psych-up cheer, and then they all lined up to start.

Annabelle breathed in the familiar chlorine-filled air, focused on those steady black lines at the bottom of the pool, and visualized herself diving in at just the right time. Making everybody forget the last race.

When the buzzer went off, Kayla got out to an easy lead, and Ruby pulled farther ahead on her leg. Annabelle's heart rate slowed down. Her team's second-best relay group was ahead of both groups from the other team.

Colette had told her not to think about leaving the blocks early—to approach the start the way she always had. But when Ruby touched the wall at the end of her leg, Annabelle was cautious. As long as she didn't get DQ'd again, this was an easy win, so she might as well play it safe.

When they won the race, they all high-fived and Colette told them good job, but when Annabelle turned to walk away, Colette called out to her.

"Hey. You have to trust yourself, okay?"

And Annabelle felt as if she'd let the team down and lost them the race, even though they'd won by half the length of the pool.

"I'll do better next time," she said, and Coach Colette nodded.

"I know."

And in Annabelle's individual races, she did. It was easier to dive off the starting blocks right when the buzzer went off instead of waiting for someone else to reach the wall. She couldn't quite forget about the risk of diving in early, but she could measure her own start off of the swimmers on either side of her. She dared herself to be the first one into the water—the way she and Mia used to dare each other to try flips and back dives off the diving board—and each time, she was. She won both individual races she swam in, which meant that she earned six more points for the team, all by herself.

The score wasn't close, but it felt good to win by a lot. And they still had a chance at making it to the Labor Day Invitational as long as they could win most of their other meets and beat South Shore when they saw them again in August.

Annabelle wrapped herself up in a plain navy towel—no more monogrammed purple for her, even though Mom kept setting that one out as if Annabelle had forgotten she had it. The middle school meet was after the high school one this time. Jeremy was talking to some of the boys, but Mia grabbed Annabelle's arm and dragged her away from the group before it started.

"Are people going out?" she asked.

Annabelle didn't know what she meant at first.

"You know," Mia said. "Like Kayla or Elisa or anyone? I've heard people sometimes hang out at night after they win a meet. Did you hear about any plans?"

Annabelle glanced over at her teammates. Kayla was talking with Ruby, and Colette was showing Elisa something on her clipboard. Connor said something to Jordan, who laughed his obnoxious seagull laugh.

"I haven't heard about anything," she said.

"Boo." Mia wrinkled up her nose and then picked at one of her fingernails. They were bright pink.

Annabelle felt a pang, thinking of their old movie-and-manicure nights. Usually at Mia's house, where Mia's mom made the best Greek dishes—spanakopita and souvlaki with tzatziki sauce—even though Mia begged for pizza. And where the TV was twice the size of Annabelle's, and there was a cushiony extra bed right there in Mia's room.

She almost asked if Mia wanted to have a sleepover tonight. It had been so long since they'd had one, and maybe it *would* feel right to talk to Mia about her dad's letter if it was only the two of them, eating those soft chocolate chip cookies out of the box and painting each other's nails and talking and talking instead of paying attention to whatever movie they'd chosen.

But then Mia leaned in close to whisper.

"Connor and I were both in line at the snack stand the day you weren't at practice, and we started talking about lacrosse. Did you know he plays?"

Annabelle opened her mouth, but no noise came out.

"He said maybe we could throw the ball around sometime after swim practice or something."

She said it like she thought Annabelle would be excited about it. Like this was something fun they could share, the way they'd shared a crush on a cute actor and gone to see his movie together last summer.

"Come on, Mia!" the middle school coach yelled.

"I guess you'd better go," Annabelle said. "Good luck."

She squeezed her balled-up swim cap in her hand as she headed toward the locker room. She told herself Connor didn't really want to throw around a lacrosse ball with Mia. Or if he did, it didn't mean anything.

But right now, he was chatting with that pretty college-aged lifeguard, and when Ruby stopped to talk to him, he put his arm around her shoulder.

So maybe it didn't mean anything that he talked about lacrosse with Mia . . . but then maybe it *also* didn't matter that he'd offered Annabelle a ride to practice or flicked her ponytail twice or watched her walk by with that look in his eyes that made her belly go hot-chocolate warm.

Maybe he flirted with *everybody* and made *everybody* feel that warm and special.

Mia's cousin had said it was a good thing if the person you liked was nice to everybody, not just you. But it had to be even better if that person was nice to everybody but even *nicer* to you.

Right when she'd almost convinced herself that maybe Connor *wasn't* extra nice to her, a hand tapped her shoulder, and when she turned around, there he was. Connor. No shirt. Gym shorts over his racing suit, slightly sunburned chest, and messy, half-dry blond hair.

There were pink marks around his green eyes where his goggles had dug into his skin. Everybody got goggle lines after racing, and Annabelle hated how they looked on her own face. But that hot-chocolate warmth filled her belly as she imagined reaching out and touching those reddish indents on Connor's.

She *shouldn't* want to touch someone else's goggle indents, but with Connor . . . there was something about those marks that made him seem the tiniest bit vulnerable. Imperfect. And somehow that made her heart swell with so much affection she couldn't believe it still fit behind her ribs.

"Nice races, HB," he said.

"You too," she squeaked out. "Your backstroke's been incredible. You've been, like, *flying.*"

That had sounded weird, maybe. Like she was trying too hard to compliment him. But Connor's grin was extra wide.

Jordan joined him then. "Way to race, kid."

Ugh. *Kid?*

But then Connor said, "Bye, Annabelle."

She loved the way her name sounded coming out of his mouth. He said it carefully, like it was in a foreign language and it mattered to him to get every sound right.

He said it like *she* mattered to him. A whole lot more than Mia or Ruby or the lifeguard or anybody else.

Chapter 17

Mom and Mitch both had work events that night, so they left Annabelle money to order dinner. She was picking up her phone to call for pizza when the text came in.

Connor.

She dropped the phone, and it bounced off one of the couch cushions and onto the ground. It buzzed a second time before she could find it.

A bunch of us from the team are going to the creamery if you wanna come.

Getting there in 30.

Annabelle's smile spread so wide that her lips nearly split in the front where she bit them when she was nervous. This *had* to mean something, Connor going out of his way to invite her.

Cool. See you there, she typed back, her fingers shaking so much that she almost dropped the phone *again*. She put in an exclamation point and a smiley face at first, then deleted them.

She texted Mom to say she was biking to get food instead of ordering, which wasn't a lie exactly, and then she added that she might get ice cream with Mia, which was.

She *could* have been getting ice cream with Mia, if she told Mia about meeting Connor and the rest of the team. But the truth was, she didn't want Mia there. So she put away her phone without sending another message.

Annabelle locked up her bike a few blocks from the Creamery. The line looped around the corner, like it always did in the summer.

What did "meeting at the Creamery" mean, exactly? There wasn't any room to hang out inside when it was this crowded. Was she supposed to find the whole group so they could wait in line together? Or order her ice cream by herself and go find them outside?

She tried to make herself walk normally, even though she had no idea what to do with her arms or how to scan the crowd for the rest of the group without looking like some pathetic girl who couldn't stand to be on her own.

At the end of the line, there was a family with two men and two little kids, and then there were a bunch of older guys wearing those faded T-shirts that are already faded when you buy them. Annabelle took a spot at the back and pretended to check something on her phone.

"Hey!" Jeremy rushed up, with Kayla a few steps behind him.

"What are you doing here?" Annabelle asked.

"Uh, same as you, I'm guessing," Jeremy teased. "Getting ice cream."

"Thanks to your generous sister who let you tag along," Kayla added.

"Mom made her bring me," Jeremy fake-whispered.

Kayla gave him a little shove, but it was a jokey shove. Kayla and Jeremy didn't fight for real the way lots of siblings seemed to.

Kayla held up her phone. "Ruby says they're almost at the front of the line and we should meet them. You guys coming, or you want to wait?"

Annabelle scanned the line in front of her. She hated when people saved spots so their friends could cut.

"Maybe we'll stay back here and meet you outside?" Jeremy said.

He looked at Annabelle to see if that's what she wanted, too. But she didn't need Jeremy to answer for her. And if Connor was up there with Ruby, she wasn't about to get stuck back here.

"I'm coming," Annabelle said.

She ignored the annoyed looks from the dads with little kids as she and Kayla pushed their way forward, and she ignored the way Jeremy kept saying, "Excuse me, I'm so sorry." It wasn't like she'd *told* him to follow her.

But when they reached Ruby, she was only with a couple of other girls from the team. No Connor. No Elisa, either.

Annabelle and Jeremy always used to order a large cup with half peanut butter cup for her and half double-chocolate chunk for him because it was cheaper than two separate small cups and the same amount of ice cream. But she was afraid Ruby would make a thing of it if they shared a cup of ice cream now, so she said, "Okay if we each get our own?" and Jeremy shrugged but didn't complain.

After they got their orders and walked outside, she finally saw Connor, sitting with Jordan on one of the gray wooden benches along the street. "You made it!" he called. He didn't clarify who he meant when he said "you." Was he talking to all of them, or mostly to her? Had he texted Kayla and Ruby and the other girls, too?

"My legs are suuuuper tired. I need a seat," Ruby whined. She plopped herself down in between Connor and Jordan, just assuming they'd scoot over so she would fit, and they did.

"Aww, poor Rubes," Connor said.

The next bench opened up, and Kayla and the other girls sat down. That only left Jeremy and Annabelle standing there.

"Curb?" Jeremy asked.

Annabelle looked at Connor again and then at Kayla and the others, but it was kind of pathetic, standing there waiting to be included. So she and Jeremy found a spot a few feet away from the benches.

Jeremy glanced over at Kayla before he sat. He'd done that a lot ever since she'd come back from her treatment program last summer: checked on what she was eating and whether she was having fun.

When Kayla had first come home, Jeremy had told Annabelle that it wasn't easy for her to eat as many calories as she was supposed to, and sometimes breakfast went on for ages because she had to work so hard to eat all the food. Annabelle wondered if it was still tough for Kayla that the plans people made to hang out usually involved eating. Tonight, Kayla had gotten sorbet instead of ice cream, and Annabelle had noticed that in a way she knew she wouldn't have if it was someone else ordering, which she felt sort of guilty about.

Kayla stuck her tongue out at Jeremy, and he stuck his tongue out back. Then he plopped down right smack next to Annabelle, and she slid away a tiny bit, so Ruby and Jordan and Connor wouldn't get the wrong idea.

"No Pricey tonight?" Connor asked Kayla, and Kayla hesitated a second before saying, "Um, I think she's with some people she works with at Beach Buzz."

Then Connor started talking to Ruby and Jordan, so Annabelle figured she might as well talk to Jeremy.

"How were your races today?" she asked.

He looked down into his ice cream. "I had a PR in the 50 free."

Annabelle stopped mid-bite. "That's great! Why didn't you text me?"

He shrugged. "It's still not that fast a time."

"Whatever," Annabelle said. "It's a big deal to beat your own record!"

He went to push his hair away from his eyes, even though it still wasn't long enough to reach his eyebrows.

Annabelle remembered how it had felt in sixth-grade science when Jeremy and Mrs. Mattson had told her she asked smart questions—how that was better than when someone told her what a great swimmer she was or called her pretty, because they were compliment-ing her for something she didn't already feel good about, deep down.

"Seriously," she said. "It's extra impressive since the other team wasn't very good. I bet you'll be able to swim even faster when the competition is stronger."

Over on the bench, Connor laughed, and Annabelle turned her head. Was it Ruby who had made him laugh like that? Or only Jordan?

"You swam well, too," Jeremy said. "I mean, obviously."

A mosquito buzzed between Annabelle and Jeremy, and they both went to swat it. Annabelle laughed as their hands knocked into each other and then checked to see if Connor had noticed. He was busy listening to some-thing Jordan was saying, though.

Jeremy finished his ice cream and tipped the cup toward him so he could slurp up the melted liquid. It got all over his mouth before he pulled a napkin from his pocket and wiped it off. Annabelle thought of Mia, who would have teased Jeremy about how his lips were cov-ered in chocolate lipstick if she were here.

"Hey, so I know I already asked you this same thing once," Annabelle started, scooping out a bite with a big piece of peanut butter cup.

"You don't want me to tell Mia about tonight," he said.

She let the bite fall off her spoon. "How did you know that's what I was going to say?"

Jeremy shrugged. "'Cause you didn't want her there that day at the pool. And . . . how things have been with you guys."

"How things have been with us?" Annabelle echoed.

Things *had* been weird—she knew they had. But she didn't like the idea that Jeremy had noticed. Or, even worse, that Mia might have said something to him.

And if Jeremy was hanging out with just her and not saying anything about it to Mia, did that mean he was also hanging out with just Mia and not saying anything about it to her?

Jeremy balled up his napkin and pressed it into the bottom of his empty ice cream cup. "Well, yeah. I mean—"

But Annabelle never got to hear the rest, because Jordan stood up from the bench. "You know what I could go for?" he called out. "A nice, refreshing dip. Who's in?"

Connor stood up, too. "Let's do it!"

Annabelle looked at Jeremy, who shrugged. She felt that same surge of frustration as she had when he kept apologizing to everyone they cut in line. It was annoying how often Jeremy shrugged. Had he always shrugged this much?

"I'm in," she said, pushing herself up off the curb.

Chapter 18

Annabelle had assumed Jordan meant they'd run down to the ocean. There was a beach just down the hill from where they were eating their ice cream. She figured they'd wade partway in. Maybe go in up to their knees, or far enough to get the bottoms of their shorts wet.

"It's less than a mile up the road," Jordan announced. "And Dennis and his wife are gone for the weekend."

"Wait, Dennis *Martin*?" Annabelle asked.

The famous movie guy? The one Jordan and Ruby had been talking about the other week at the pool?

Jordan pointed at her. "Ding ding ding!"

"What about that huge fence?" Ruby asked, and Jordan wiggled his eyebrows.

"I know the code."

"Dennis Martin gave *you* the code?" Connor asked.

"Well, technically his wife gave it to the pool guy. But I was listening! And I happen to know their security system's busted, because I *also* heard her setting up an appointment for somebody to come fix it next week."

"Nice," Connor said, clapping Jordan on the back. "Well done, man."

Ruby was practically jumping up and down. "I can't believe we're going to swim in Dennis Martin's pool!" She squeezed one of Jordan's arms and one of Connor's, which was just greedy. Shouldn't she at least have to choose? And how were they going to swim in a pool when none of them had bathing suits? Were they going to swim in their clothes? Or—*ack*—not in their clothes?

"This seems like a pretty bad idea," Jeremy whispered as the whole group started the trek across the street.

He and Annabelle were at the very back, and Annabelle was thinking the same thing: This seemed like a *terrible* idea. Especially after Ruby took out one of those e-cigarettes. In theory, Annabelle knew there were high school kids who vaped or smoked or whatever. But she'd never actually been hanging out with any of them when they did, and now the ice cream she'd rushed to finish churned in her belly.

Kayla hung back to wait. "You guys should bike home now," she whispered.

Annabelle looked down the side street where she'd parked her bike, and she pictured herself safe and free, riding back home with Jeremy like they'd done a million times before. The still-warm evening air would rush through her hair as they watched the horizon go orangey-pink and talked about Bertha the shark, or what made the sky change colors at sunset, or which talking animal video was the funniest. They'd pedal themselves away from Ruby's vaping and Jordan's seagull laugh and even Connor, who thought swimming in some famous person's pool sounded like a great idea.

"Mom wouldn't want you doing this," Kayla said to Jeremy. "Your mom wouldn't either, Annabelle."

Jeremy let out a snort-laugh. "And you think Mom would want *you* breaking into some movie star's yard?"

Movie director, Annabelle thought, annoyed that Jeremy didn't know.

"It's . . ." Kayla's eyes darted up to the rest of the group. "It's different for me."

Annabelle blinked. She'd thought Kayla saw her as an actual friend, not just Jeremy's little buddy. She'd thought being on the relay team together made them more equal and it didn't matter that Kayla was three years older than she was. But maybe that did matter to Kayla after all?

Jeremy looked at Kayla for a long time, and Annabelle recognized the expression on his face. It was the same one he used to get in math class before he got moved up, when he would hold himself back from answering every single question because he didn't want to rub it in that he knew more than everybody else. He had something else to say to Kayla now, but he hadn't decided whether or not to say it.

Finally, he shook his head. "Whatever, Kay," he said, and then he turned to Annabelle. "Come on. Let's go home."

And somehow, knowing that Kayla thought she and Jeremy were too young to come along and hearing Jeremy suggest exactly what she'd just pictured doing made her change her mind.

She hadn't even gotten to talk to Connor yet, and he'd *specifically* invited her. Plus, even if Kayla didn't want *them* to go, *she* was going along with it, and she wasn't the kind of person who got in trouble. It couldn't be that terrible an idea if she was doing it.

"I think this sounds like an adventure," Annabelle said. "You can go home if you want, but I'm in."

Jeremy and Kayla sighed almost in unison.

"Fine. I'll stay, too," Jeremy said.

As if he thought Annabelle needed his protection or something. But the rest of the group was too far ahead for them to wait back here any longer, so she let it go and texted her mom that she was hanging out with Jeremy and Kayla as they all speed-walked to catch up.

At least Ruby wasn't vaping anymore by the time Annabelle squeezed herself into the pack of people, as close to Connor as she could get without seeming desperate.

"You really up for this, HB?" Connor asked.

"Oh, yeah, definitely," she said, and her voice sounded more like Mia's lacrosse-girl voice than her own. She peeked back at Jeremy, who hung a few feet behind. He kicked a pebble that bounced up and barely missed Connor's calf.

"Nice. You're the best," Connor said, reaching his hand out for a high five.

And everything inside her glowed like the sunset-striped sky that transformed all around them, vast and magical and bright.

Annabelle stayed in the middle of the group as they crossed the cobblestoned streets of town and then passed the row of fully occupied bed-and-breakfasts. Jeremy still sulked a few steps behind her with Kayla and her friends, but he had *chosen* to come along. She hadn't asked him to.

A steel-gray convertible sped by, kicking up the sand along the side of the road.

"My dad has a car like that," Ruby said. "I thought

he'd let me practice driving on it, but no. I'm getting my mom's old Volvo, since it has better safety ratings, even though the convertible's fine for *him* to drive."

Connor glanced past Ruby, toward Annabelle. Their eyes locked for a split second, and he raised his eyebrows. Annabelle knew what that look meant.

Ruby was a summer person, and getting her mom's hand-me-down expensive car was a summer person problem. Annabelle and Connor were on the inside of something in that moment. Ruby was outside of it, and she didn't even know.

After a few minutes, Connor and Jordan started talking about some rumor involving people from Gray Island High who Annabelle didn't know but Ruby somehow did.

Annabelle didn't want to be like those bobbing seals at Bluff Point, waiting for any tiny opening so they could push their way up onto the rocks. Behind her, Kayla and the other girls were talking about someone's sweet-sixteen party—a party Jeremy definitely wasn't invited to and definitely didn't have any interest in discussing.

Connor's attention was now 100 percent focused on whatever juicy thing Jordan was saying, so she slowed her pace, falling into step with Jeremy.

"Hey."

"Hey." He kicked another pebble.

And yeah, it had technically been his choice to stay, but it wouldn't have been all that easy to go home when nobody else was.

She sighed. "You know, we've barely gone to see the seals this summer."

When he didn't respond, she added, "We've got to go back before you leave for Boston next week for your program. Get some more Bluff Point time in."

He still didn't say anything, so she elbowed his arm gently.

"Remember the Mia seal last summer?"

One day they'd watched an especially blubbery seal lie out in exactly the same position as Mia: on its belly with its little flippers bouncing up and down the same way Mia bounced her feet. Jeremy had taken video on his phone, going back and forth filming one and then the other, and he'd added hilarious music in the background.

Mia had thought it was just as funny as Jeremy and Annabelle had, when they'd showed it to her. She almost never got offended when people teased her, which is probably why she was so good at teasing other people.

"Maybe Sunday," Jeremy said.

"Deal," Annabelle replied. "Maybe . . . um . . . maybe

Mia will come, too. Unless you think she wouldn't want to? If you think she's mad at me?"

"I think she just misses you on the swim team." Jeremy sped through the explanation too fast, as if it wouldn't be so obvious that the words weren't true if he said them quickly enough. Or that they weren't the *whole* truth, anyway.

Annabelle was about to ask more, but then the whole group walked up to the edge of Ashton Road—a road their parents wouldn't let them bike on even during the day because there was a turn so sharp you couldn't see cars coming. Annabelle felt a pang, thinking about what her mom would say if she knew what was happening.

But the sky still glowed bright, and the night was quiet except for the sounds of their talking and the chirp of crickets. They would be able to hear a car for sure.

Jeremy's head darted back and forth as he searched for headlights, and he picked up his pace in the middle of the road and grabbed Annabelle's wrist to pull her along with him as they crossed.

Annabelle jerked free. "Whoa. Relax."

Jeremy drew back a little, as if her words had stung. But seriously: She could handle crossing a street by herself.

"Here we are!" Jordan announced as they approached an enormous house with a towering iron fence.

Annabelle bit down on her bottom lip as Jordan stepped up to enter the code. They were really doing this. She had known where they were going, of course, but she'd almost let herself forget.

Jeremy caught her eye, and she had to look away so all his nervousness wouldn't crash into hers.

When Jordan punched in the numbers, the keypad beeped once and lit up red. He cursed and Ruby groaned, but Annabelle's nerves began to calm down.

"We can't get in?" she said, trying her best to sound disappointed.

"Patience, grasshopper," Jordan replied.

Everyone else laughed, so Annabelle did, too.

"Got a plan B?" Connor asked.

"Let me think about it," Jordan said.

Connor narrowed his green eyes and tapped his chin to show he was thinking. "I have an idea. If Hummingbird's game."

And *boom*, Annabelle's heart thudded against her rib cage. "Sure," she said, even though she had no clue what he was about to suggest.

Connor put one hand on either side of her waist, and she let out a yelp as he lifted her off the ground. Hanging there in the air, she was aware of every individual rib his fingers touched.

"Yeah, she weighs nothing," he said, setting her down. "Plus, look how long her arms are. If we lift her up high enough to grab onto the top, she can pull herself over and let the rest of us in."

The breeze had cooled down enough that Kayla and Ruby had both put on sweatshirts, but warmth spread throughout Annabelle's body. Kayla's forehead crinkled up with concern, but Annabelle didn't let that bother her. She felt dainty and desirable and important. Connor needed *her* for this plan. Everybody did.

Connor stood on Annabelle's left side, and Jordan stepped up to her right. They counted, "One, two, three," and then Annabelle was in the air, higher than when only Connor had lifted her. They pushed her toward the fence, and her elbow banged against an iron bar.

"Grab on!" someone called, and Annabelle tried to ignore the brief, clanging pain in her arm. She reached out and up—her fingertips grazed the top bar, but she wasn't high enough to grab on.

"I can't quite . . ." she started, and Connor and Jordan grunted as they heaved her higher—high enough so that she could see over the fence, into the yard. She pushed herself forward, hooking her arms over the top. She winced as one of the pointy iron pillars scraped her right forearm, but as she adjusted her grip, she yelled out, "Got it!"

And right then, the security alarm started blaring, drowning out her voice.

Chapter 19

"Run!" a girl's voice screamed. Ruby, it sounded like. Then there were footsteps. Lots of them, pounding away from Annabelle.

"I thought you said the security system was broken!" Connor said.

"It was!"

Jordan's laugh blared over the screeching alarm, like this was all some kind of joke. He let go of Annabelle, taking off after the others, and her right shoulder dipped without his support.

Then Connor said, "We've gotta get out of here. Come back down!"

And he let go, too. As if she could slide down the iron fence and follow. He must have thought she could. He wouldn't have stepped away if he hadn't. But she was up too high.

She let go with one arm—the scratched-up right one, with its sore elbow. She reached for something lower down that she could hang on to, but her fingertips only hit air. Her left arm ached from holding all her weight. Maybe the ground wasn't so far away after all. If she let herself drop, she'd probably land on her feet.

She took three deep breaths, and then she let go.

Her left knee smacked one of the iron bars halfway down, and her right ankle twisted under her weight when her foot hit the ground. But that was nothing compared to the pain that knifed through her right wrist when she put down her hand to stop her fall.

She had to get herself up.

The alarm still wailed above her head, and somebody would show up soon. Some security officer or the police, and she'd be the only one there. She pressed one scraped palm into the ground and tried to straighten her legs, but everything was throbbing. Her hands, her knees, her ankle, and her wrist most of all.

But then she heard them. Footsteps, running in the right direction. Toward her. Connor had come back!

Except she could see reflective patches from some-body's sneakers, and Connor was wearing sandals. And when she made out a flash of hair under the streetlights, it was brown, not blond.

Jeremy.

Relief flooded her, followed by disappointment so huge it muffled the pain in her wrist. She could cry in front of Jeremy, that was the good thing. And he was the smartest person she knew. He would figure out what to do to keep them both safe. But if Jeremy was the one coming back to get her, that meant Connor wasn't.

"Annabelle," Jeremy said. "I can't believe those dicks left you!"

Jeremy spat out the word *dicks*. It sounded way too harsh, way too . . . obscene coming out of his mouth. He *never* talked like that.

She stiffened. "Don't call them that."

"Your knee's bleeding. And your hands."

He leaned down so she could hook her arm over his shoulder, and he helped her get up. She smelled his shampoo, almost but not quite covering the scent of chlorine.

"What hurts the most?" he said into her ear. Softly, the same way he'd whispered questions and instructions when they were partners on a sixth-grade science field trip and he didn't want to scare away the seagulls they were observing.

"My wrist." She held it up. "And this ankle's not great either."

He punched a text message into his phone and then switched to her other side, so that her hurt ankle was closer to him and she could put less weight on it.

"Hurry!" she said. "We're going to get caught!"

"I don't want to hurt you even more."

Too slowly, as the alarm kept wailing, he helped her hobble away. When they got to the side of Ashton Road, he hoisted her onto his back. The sky was getting dark fast now. She could feel his frantic heartbeat where her hands hung onto his chest, and she slipped partway down his back as he ran across the street. As soon as they were on the other side, he put her down, panting. "Hang on a second."

His phone dinged, and he sent a reply text and then shoved it back into his pocket. Kayla, probably.

Annabelle pulled her phone out of her pocket, too, and sure enough, there was a group text from Kayla to her and Jeremy.

Are you guys OK?? So sorry we lost you!! Where are you??

But nothing from Connor. And no group reply from Jeremy, either.

"Wait, who are you texting?" Annabelle asked, but Jeremy didn't answer. He bent down in front of her a little so she could climb on his back, and she got a flash of her dad, years ago, crouching down the same way and carrying her around piggyback or up on his shoulders whenever they were in a crowd and she got tired.

"I think I can walk by myself," she said, because the pain in her ankle was shrinking now. But her wrist was only getting worse.

When they made it back to the edge of town, Jeremy stopped next to a bench in front of the first bed-and-breakfast and pulled out his phone again.

"Seriously, who are you texting?" Annabelle asked.

Jeremy frowned. "Your wrist is swollen already."

It had puffed up pretty badly, and the tender skin on the side of her thumb was turning blue.

"Is Kayla coming back for us?" she asked, pointing at Jeremy's phone. "Or . . . um. The rest of them?"

Jeremy shook his head. "My mom is. She'll meet us right here, and we can pick up our bikes on the way back."

Annabelle's throat went dry. "What did you tell your mom?"

"I told her where we are, so she can get us."

Annabelle let out a long, shaky breath. "Were you texting your mom this whole time?"

"Uh-huh." Jeremy's fingertips brushed against his forehead, pushing aside the hair that wasn't there anymore. Once he remembered, he ran his hand over the top of his head instead.

"Where did you say we were? Back when you first texted?"

"On Ashton, heading toward town. She said to text as soon as we were someplace safe to stop, and she'd come."

Jeremy looked at Annabelle, brown eyes wide and a little desperate. Her face must have told him he'd done something wrong, but despite all of those A-pluses, he didn't seem to understand what.

"How are we going to explain why we were on Ashton Street?" she asked.

Even if there really wasn't any surveillance footage, if their parents knew they'd been on a street they were supposed to stay away from and then word got out that someone had attempted to break into Dennis Martin's property, it wouldn't be hard to connect the dots.

What if, thanks to her and Jeremy, the entire group got in trouble? Kayla and Connor and everyone?

"You were hurt!" Jeremy protested. "You needed help, and I didn't know what to do!"

"So you texted your *mom*?" Annabelle was nearly shouting. She didn't mean to shout, but her wrist was still throbbing, and when she checked her phone again, the text from Kayla was the only one there. Nothing from Connor, *still*.

"Sorry for trying to help you," Jeremy snapped. He moved to the far edge of the bench, as if he couldn't handle being near her.

This was *Jeremy*, who had collected quartz stones and examined seagull nests with her in sixth-grade science. Who kept on swimming the end of a lap of breaststroke, over and over, just so she could practice her start. Whose eyes lit up when he talked about Bertha the white shark. He was her friend, and he had come back for her.

She started to scooch over toward him, but then he added, "Sorry for being the *only* one who tried. Unlike Connor Madison, who just let you get hurt and then didn't bother to check on you!"

He spat out Connor's name like it was a bad word, and every single muscle in her body tensed.

"He didn't know I was hurt! If you'd replied to Kayla instead of texting your *mom*, they all would have known and they could have come to find us! They're probably looking for us right now!"

An angry glare transformed Jeremy's features. Annabelle's mom always said what a sweet face Jeremy had, and Annabelle knew what she meant. There was something about how fast his smile came and how round and heavily lashed his eyes were—it was obvious from the first time you saw him that Jeremy was someone who'd never be cruel.

But it was not a sweet face that looked at Annabelle right now.

"Go ahead and text them, then," Jeremy said. "Go find out for yourself how much Connor cares."

He let out a mean little laugh after he said it. The kind of laugh that said, "How stupid are you, Annabelle?" She'd heard it from other kids sometimes when a teacher called on her even though she didn't want to be called on and she said something really, really wrong. But she'd never heard it from Jeremy before now.

She blinked back the tears that pricked her eyes. "Fine. I will."

First, she texted Kayla, who wrote right back to say she was so sorry Annabelle had fallen and then called Jeremy. He took a few steps away to take the call, and all Annabelle could hear were his whispered promises that he wouldn't say anything to his mom that would get Kayla in trouble.

Annabelle stared at the display on her phone, but it only showed the time and the old background picture of her and Mia blowing kisses at the camera.

Connor would have no idea she was hurt unless she told him. He might assume she and Jeremy had decided they'd rather hang out, just the two of them. He might think she *like*-liked Jeremy. She had to text him, she realized.

I'm a little banged up but OK, she wrote.

She dug her fingernails into the raw skin of her left palm again and bit back a scream. *Ruby* was probably with Connor right now, cozying up to him and trying to make him forget Annabelle's black bathing suit and how easy she was to lift high in the air.

Are you guys OK? she added.

And then, so he knew and didn't have to wonder, **I'm getting a ride home.**

And finally, **Sorry for not catching up.**

Then Mrs. Green's car pulled up. When she saw Annabelle, she said, "Oh, sweetie," and made Jeremy help Annabelle into the back seat and then load her bike onto the rack when they stopped to get it.

As they drove back to their neighborhood, Mrs. Green kept glancing over at Jeremy and then checking on Annabelle in the rearview mirror, and Annabelle kept staring at her phone, waiting for a text that never came.

Chapter 20

At home, Mom and Mitch popped up from the living room couch as soon as they saw Annabelle.

"Oh, honey, what happened?" Mom said.

"I . . . I fell," Annabelle said, blinking back tears and cradling her hand.

"On your bike?" Mom asked. "Where? Why didn't you call? How did you get home?"

"Mrs. Green brought me," Annabelle said. "It wasn't on my bike. I fell in town."

Dennis Martin's house *was* in town, technically. She didn't want to lie, because then everything would be even worse if Mrs. Green told Mom and Mitch where she and Jeremy had been. But she was hoping Mom and Mitch would assume she'd tripped on a loose cobblestone near the Creamery or something.

Mom took out the rubbing alcohol and Neosporin for the scrapes on Annabelle's knee, arm, and hands, and Mitch wrapped an ice pack around her wrist.

"Maybe it won't be quite so bad in the morning," Mom said.

Maybe.

Maybe after Annabelle had iced her wrist and elevated it on a pillow all night, it would go back to its usual size. It'd be a little sore, but she could deal with soreness. Ever since she'd started swimming seriously, at least one part of her body had been sore at all times.

And maybe Connor would text her back any minute. Or call, even.

But he didn't.

The next morning, she didn't have a single new text or call. Her wrist and thumb were even bigger, and the tender skin was pink and purple, like the ugliest sunset imaginable. She couldn't rotate her hand at all. She could barely even flex her fingers.

When she came down the stairs, she expected Mitch and Mom to scramble up to help her again—to make a fuss asking what they could get her to eat and holding out ice packs and ibuprofen.

But neither of them budged from their places at the kitchen table. Slowly and almost in unison, their heads turned toward her, and the expressions on their faces matched. If she were a word person like Jeremy, she'd know how to describe the way they looked at her. It was something worse than disappointed. Something bigger than mad.

Could there have been surveillance footage after all? Could somebody from the security company have called somehow? Or the police, even?

"I can explain." She scrambled for a story, but how could she possibly explain what she was doing attempting to climb the fence outside some famous person's yard? She could claim that Jordan had left something important there when he was mowing the lawn? His wallet, maybe. Or his phone. No, an inhaler. She'd been helping, because he needed it right away.

"We heard from Mrs. Green this morning," Mom said.

Annabelle lowered herself into a chair. Not the police, at least, but not good.

"She couldn't get the whole story out of Jeremy," Mom started. "But he said something about you getting hurt because of something you were doing with a high school boy who just left you after you fell?"

That phrase got stuck inside Annabelle's head and bounced around there. *Just left you. Just left you. Just left you.*

"I . . . We were all hanging out together," Annabelle said. "Me and Jeremy and . . ." She wasn't going to be the one to tell on Kayla if Jeremy hadn't. "And a bunch of other people. And they . . . It was nobody's fault. I fell and we got separated and they didn't realize I was hurt."

That wasn't quite right anymore, though. They *did* know, after she'd texted Connor. Or he did, anyway. But he probably thought it wasn't that bad, since she hadn't made a big thing about it. Maybe she should have made it sound more serious?

"We trusted you, Annabelle," Mom said. "I was afraid swimming with high school kids would be too much for you to handle."

"It isn't!" Annabelle insisted.

"Was it that Madison kid?" Mitch asked. "Connor? I don't like the kind of attention he gives you. I've seen him talking to you way too much when I pick you up from practice."

For a split second, that thrilled Annabelle—the idea that Connor's attention was so obvious that even Mitch had noticed.

But then Mitch got up from his seat and paced around the kitchen. His whole face was red. His neck, too. He was wearing a light green shirt, and his face and neck clashed with it.

"He's not . . . It's not . . ." Annabelle started.

"No high school boy should be paying that kind of attention to you," Mitch boomed, and Annabelle jumped. She'd heard him yell at his own daughters before but never at her. "You're a *kid*."

And now that phrase joined in with the other one, bouncing around inside her skull and jarring her every time they collided.

You're a kid. You're a kid. Just left you. You're a kid.

"You lied to us about who you were with last night," Mom said. "You knew the deal, Annabelle. No more high school team now. When you're all healed up, you can go back and swim with the middle school."

"What?" Annabelle squeaked, but Mom held up one hand.

"You had one strike left after missing tutoring. This was a big strike, Annabelle. We trusted you."

Annabelle looked at Mitch, sure he'd fight for her. He might be mad, but he knew how important it was for her to stay on the team. She was sure he'd remind Mom that a person was supposed to get *three* strikes, that's how strikes worked—but he only shook his head.

"I'll call Colette this afternoon," Mom said. "She'll understand that this won't work out. That you're just not ready."

It was the meanest thing Mom could have said.

Because yes—when Annabelle had found out she'd disqualified the relay team, when Connor had commented on her personalized towel, and when Ruby had taken out her e-cigarette—in those moments, Annabelle hadn't felt like she belonged on the high school team. But then there were other moments—when Connor flicked her ponytail and lifted her up over his head, when Elisa and Kayla talked to her like she was one of them, when Coach Colette acted like she was capable of something special—in those moments, she felt like she counted.

Swimming with the high school team, helping them win the league, even, and spending time with Connor and Kayla and Elisa—she was way more ready for those things than she was for anything else people expected her to do. She had a much better chance of doing that stuff well than of passing eighth-grade history.

Mitch took her to Urgent Care to get her wrist checked, and the doctor who took X-rays and examined her said things could be worse. She had a fracture in the lower part of her right thumb and a badly sprained right wrist. She was lucky that she was left-handed, and she didn't need an actual cast—only a splint that had to stay on all the time except when she was in the shower. She had to wear it for a month, and pretty soon she could start doing physical therapy.

"How long do you think it'll be before she can swim again?" Mitch asked.

"Light swimming should be okay in a few weeks," the doctor said.

But "light swimming" wasn't going to do Annabelle any good. Not while the rest of the team was getting to the peak of training, before they'd taper to get ready for the biggest races of the season.

Mitch didn't clarify what he was really asking, though. He probably figured there was no point, when Mom was calling Coach Colette to pull Annabelle from the high school team, anyway.

And on the drive home, he turned the radio up loud so they wouldn't have to talk.

He'd been so proud and happy so, so recently, when Colette had asked Annabelle to swim up with the high school team. But now that was over. There were no up-coming meets for them to strategize about. There was no point in breaking down some element of her stroke.

Without swimming, everything between the two of them was even more broken than her messed-up hand. Without swimming, she and Mitch didn't have anything to say to each other at all.

But just when the tears had pooled in Annabelle's eyes, her phone chirped, and there it was: what she'd been waiting and waiting for. A message from Connor. Finally.

Even though Mitch was focused on the road, she shielded her phone the way kids shielded their test papers at school.

Sorry for not texting before, he wrote. **And sorry we couldn't find you.**

Couldn't find her. So he must have tried!

Battery was dying and everything was chaos!

And then he wrote, **See you at practice Monday?** With a smiley face. Like he was hoping he would.

Annabelle didn't tell him about being off the team for good, but when she wrote back about her wrist and thumb, he sent back a string of sad emojis.

She looked at them for the whole rest of the drive home, letting those tiny yellow faces parade through her mind and block out the memory of Jeremy's angry face from the night before and Mom's and Mitch's worse-than-angry ones from this morning.

Chapter 21

Annabelle was in so much trouble that she was barely allowed to leave the house. There was no way she would have been able to go see the seals at Bluff Point on Sunday with Jeremy even if he'd still wanted to, which she was sure he didn't. But at least Mom said she could take her summer reading book and walk down to the little residents-only beach at the end of the unpaved side road that split off from their street. The place where she, Mom, and Mitch sometimes went to watch the sunset and Mitch took out his little boat for a sail.

"I'll come check on you in a little bit!" Mom said, because she was keeping tabs on Annabelle's every move.

The side road wasn't paved, but the sand was packed down hard from cars driving over it. As Annabelle reached the dunes, it turned as soft and fine as the powdered sugar Mitch used to dust the tops of waffles when he made them for breakfast on the weekends.

The morning sun baked the metal and black fabric of her wrist brace, so she plopped down in the sand a few feet away from the dunes, slid off the brace, and let her swollen hand rest on the warm pillow the sand made.

The little beach was a protected bay, which meant the water was always calm. Tiny ripples wrinkled the glassy surface and lapped against the shore, and long piles of dried brown seaweed stretched across the sand. The Bennetts from next door were out playing. Mrs. Bennett stood at the edge of the water, watching little Kelsey squeal and splash as she ran a few steps out and then back. But Mr. Bennett was out pretty far. Julia, Kelsey's older sister, was holding onto a kickboard and kicking her way to him over the tiny ripple-waves.

"Almost here!" he called. "You can do it!"

Annabelle's legs itched to jump into the water and show Julia how to make her kicks more efficient—by slowing them down and letting her feet sink deeper instead of skimming the surface and sending up so much splash.

Annabelle didn't usually swim for real in the ocean—she mostly just waded out to the sandbar here or rode in the waves at Bluff Point and saved her real strokes for the pool.

But today, if her wrist and thumb didn't ache, she would have loved to wade out to the sandbar and then keep on swimming as far as she could go. All the way out past the protected cove, toward the rocky open ocean.

And as she sat there looking out at the water, she remembered something she hadn't thought of in ages. From back before Mom had met Mitch, before Annabelle had even heard of Gray Island. Back when she, Mom, and Dad had gone down to the Jersey Shore for a week one summer.

They'd gone to the beach early in the morning, before it got crowded. The water had been calm, and she and Dad had kicked their way out to a buoy. Annabelle had been propped up on a boogie board while her dad had crawled along, never putting his face in the water, so she'd never feel alone.

"It's too far," she'd protested. "I can barely even see it."

"You're doing great," Dad had said. "But if you get tired, we'll turn around. Any time. Just say the word."

Her legs did get tired, but not until they were so close to the buoy that she could see the black stripes on top. She couldn't turn around now, when they'd gotten this close, but the farther she kept going, the farther she'd have to kick her way back.

"I'll pull you in if you need me to," Dad said.

And knowing that she had a backup plan was enough to power her out to the spot.

There was nothing magical about the place where the buoy sat—no real reason why the view from that floating red sphere should have been any more special than the view from five or ten feet behind it. It probably wasn't even *that* far out, or the lifeguards wouldn't have let them go.

But Annabelle and Dad stayed out there for a few minutes, treading water as they looked out at the vast horizon and then back at the beach. It took a minute to find Mom, who sat way back near the dunes with a big straw sunhat and a book propped on her knees. She seemed smaller than usual, as if Annabelle were peering at her through the wrong end of a pair of binoculars.

Annabelle felt stronger and bigger than she ever had but also more aware of how giant the ocean was—how giant the whole *world* was—and how tiny she and her parents were in comparison.

She didn't need her dad to pull her on the way back. She managed to kick almost the whole way, and then she rode in on a wave at the end, just like he had taught her that same trip. She gave into the ocean's power, letting it push her toward the shore.

Now Julia Bennett was kicking her way back in with her dad walking beside her, the water barely up to his waist.

He was a good dad, Mr. Bennett. Cheerful and friendly, and he never seemed to yell, even when he was telling Julia and Kelsey to come inside and they didn't listen.

But her dad had been a good dad too, for a long time.

Maybe now he was back to that old version of himself, who gave her piggyback rides when she was tired and made her feel strong and safe enough to kick all the way out to that buoy and back.

And he knew what it was like to be bad at school. He knew what it was like to mess up and make Mom worry.

Yeah, there had been a lot of moments when she'd thought it would be easier if Mitch were her real dad. But Mitch *wasn't* her dad, and Mitch had daughters of his own, and she had no guarantee that everything could go back to that easy, cozy way it had been between them now that she had ruined her chances with swimming and made him mad instead of proud.

Here with Mom and Mitch, Annabelle was like those brand-new cedar beams on their deck—the ones that had clashed with the weathered old ones and bothered her mom so much when they'd first moved in.

She didn't fit with smart, successful Mom and Mitch, and she didn't fit at school, and now she couldn't try to fit on the high school swim team, either. And unlike those deck beams, she wouldn't get any closer to matching as time went on.

Dad was doing better, and he was nearby, and he missed her. It seemed so obvious now, that of course she should write him back. She couldn't believe she'd waited so long.

She waved goodbye to the Bennetts, told Mom it was too hot outside, and rushed up to her room, where she opened her half-filled notebook from last year's science class and started to write.

Chapter 22

Annabelle wrote the letter over and over until she got the tone right—more times than Mr. Derrickson made her rewrite the beginning of her history essays. In the end, she decided to start with easy stuff: how much she liked walking on the little beach near the cottage in the off-season, with a thermos of hot chocolate and the wind whipping her hair; how the locals got annoyed with the summer people for swooping in as soon as the sun warmed the sand but bolting before the threat of hurricanes; how the fly was still her best stroke, but she raced in free, too.

She didn't write about school or her wrist or swimming with the high school team. And she asked questions, but not too many and nothing too personal. Just how Dad liked Boston, and if he was still going to root for the Yankees even though he was now in Red Sox country.

Finally, she added a P.S.

It would be nice to come to Boston to see you. Since it's the summer, I have plenty of time.

It would be too weird to have Mom or Mitch go with her, but maybe they would let her go by herself. The ferry left from the harbor right in town, down the hill from the Creamery. She knew how to get from the ferry terminal to the bus stop on the Cape, and the bus went right to South Station in Boston. Since she sometimes went with Mia's family, she knew how to take the T around the city, too. She could even tell Mom and Mitch that she and Mia were going to visit Jeremy at his summer program but then go to Dad's instead.

She wouldn't do it, really. It would never work, when Mom insisted on checking in to see if she'd made it to tutoring at the library or when she walked five minutes down to the little beach. But she still felt a quick thrill, just knowing it would technically be possible. Just thinking about doing something that big without Mom or Mia or Jeremy or *anyone* knowing.

The next morning, when Mitch sent Annabelle outside to pick up the newspaper, she put the letter to Dad in the mailbox, facedown underneath a few bills Mom and Mitch were sending out.

Her phone rang as she walked back to the house, and she cringed when she saw the display. Mia.

They hadn't talked or texted since the meet on Friday. Mia didn't know about Annabelle's wrist or going to the Creamery with Connor. Unless Jeremy had said something to her, even though Annabelle had asked him not to?

Annabelle tried to take three breaths before she answered, but the air wouldn't come all the way in. "Hey, what's up?" she said.

"You tell me." Mia's voice was X-Acto-knife sharp again. So Jeremy must have told her about Friday night.

Annabelle tried again to steady her breathing and focus on the nearby ocean—always rolling in and out, in and out, whether Mia was furious with her or not. If she really listened, she could hear the soft swishing of the tiny waves that lapped onto the shore at the little beach down the road.

"Well, I sprained my wrist and broke my thumb," she blurted out. "And my mom and Mitch are really mad. 'Cause I went out with . . ." She paused, then decided not to mention Connor. "Jeremy and Kayla and some girls from the swim team on Friday."

Mia didn't say anything.

"I really screwed up," she added.

Mia let out a short, harsh laugh. "Yeah. I heard."

Annabelle stiffened. "What did you hear?"

"Jeremy told me about your little adventures. How

you were out gallivating with Connor and Jordan and them, even though you told me you didn't know about any plans."

Annabelle was pretty sure the word wasn't *gallivating*, and for a second she wished Jeremy were around to correct Mia. Or that she were sure enough to correct Mia herself.

"I . . . I didn't know they were going out when you asked me," she said. "It was a last-minute thing."

"And I heard you got Connor to try to lift you over the fence at Dennis Martin's house, but then he *left* when you got hurt," Mia went on.

Got Connor to lift her? It had been his idea! And he hadn't *wanted* to leave her!

Mia feels left out, Annabelle told herself. *She's upset that I didn't invite her. I can probably fix this if I figure out the right thing to say.*

Except then Mia added, "It sounds like you really treated Jeremy like crap."

"I have to go," Annabelle croaked. Because she couldn't stand the idea of Mia and Jeremy united without her. Bonding with each other by saying all sorts of awful things behind her back.

And yes, Jeremy had come back to get Annabelle and helped her back to town. But it's not like he'd been nice to her while he was doing it. And if he'd just kept his mouth shut, she'd get to go back to the high school team once her wrist and thumb healed, and she and Mia would be fine. Or maybe not fine, but not like this.

Annabelle listened again for the gentle swish of the water. Her wrist and thumb still hurt, but right now that was nothing compared to the way her muscles ached to be in the ocean or the pool—she didn't care which. She wanted to dive under for ages before she had to come up for air. To block out everything except the powerful swish, pull, and kick of her own arms and legs. To be going to practice tomorrow, where she could wear her black suit and make sure Ruby, with her flowery-smelling hair and pink bikini, didn't steal all of Connor's attention. Make sure Elisa and Kayla didn't decide to befriend Mia in her place.

The front door to her house creaked open. "Belle!" Mom called. "Come back inside, honey. You can't stand out there without any sunscreen, and you have to finish that chapter before tutoring!"

A few days ago, she'd been the girl who just might help her team win a championship and start dating an almost-sophomore.

Now she was only Annabelle: useless and hurt and alone.

She glanced back at the mailbox and wished she could somehow squeeze herself into that envelope and get mailed off to Dad's new house along with her letter.

Chapter 23

The next night, Annabelle sat up in bed with her summer reading book propped up on her knees and her still-throbbing hand resting on a pillow.

Elisa had texted her to say they'd missed her at practice and to see how her hand was doing. Kayla had, too, even though Annabelle had been afraid Kayla would be mad at her, since Jeremy was.

But then they'd both just written back with "I'm so sorry"s when she'd told them how bad the injury was, and those tiny flashes of conversation had made her feel worse, not better. They'd reminded her how bored and lonely she was . . . and they'd made her wish Connor would text, too.

She could text him, though.

He'd been the one to start all of their text conversations so far. Except the one Friday night when she'd texted to say she was okay. But that one basically didn't count, since he probably *would* have texted if things hadn't gotten so chaotic and his phone had had more battery.

A girl like Ruby wouldn't think twice about texting Connor even when he hadn't texted her first. Mia probably wouldn't either, if she had his number.

Annabelle unlocked her phone and felt that zinging, about-to-race adrenaline as she found their last conversation and started to type.

Hey. What are you up to?

Connor replied right away. **Not much. Missed you at practice today.**

Missed you! She squeezed her pillow to her chest to keep from squealing.

Hope you guys went through the door at the pool instead of climbing the fence, she wrote.

LOL, he replied, and she squeezed her pillow tighter.

Maybe swimming really wasn't the only thing she did well. Maybe she was pretty decent at this, too.

Over the next few days, Annabelle and Connor texted every night. Annabelle usually had to text first, but Connor always asked her questions—like what she had done that day, and if her hand was any better, and whether the summer people seemed more obnoxious than usual.

Every time he asked a question, she got that warm, belly-full-of-hot-chocolate feeling. Because every question he asked meant that he wanted to keep the conversation going. That he liked texting with her as much as she liked texting with him.

There was one time when he sent a text that didn't make any sense—a **haha no don't do it!** when she hadn't said anything funny, and she had no idea what he was telling her not to do. And then he followed it up with an **Oops! Sorry meant to send to someone else!** And then she had to wonder how many other people he was texting with right then, and who they were.

But Jeremy had done that to her once with a text that was supposed to go to his mom. It didn't have to mean anything.

Other than texting with Connor and wondering whether or not her dad had gotten her letter yet, she didn't have much going on except tutoring. On Friday, when the rest of the swim team had a meet on Cape Cod, she beat Janine to the library for their session and chose her favorite table—the one that looked out at the sparkling water on the horizon.

She stared out the window, wondering why the ocean seemed gray from this distance even though it was always blue or green up close and wishing she could ask Jeremy what he thought.

Jeremy, who was supposed to go straight from today's meet to Boston, since his summer program started tomorrow. Who hadn't even said goodbye.

"Hey there," Janine said, sliding into the seat across from Annabelle. "How's the wrist?"

Annabelle shrugged. "Hurts."

"It must be hard not to be able to swim, huh? When I had shin splints and couldn't run last summer it was the worst."

Janine shook her head at the memory, and Annabelle noticed that Janine's tight curls stayed put when her head moved, instead of swinging side to side the way her own hair would. Back when Janine went to the Academy, she'd worn her hair in a straight ponytail or a tight, high bun, but since she'd come back from college this spring, it was like a puffy cloud around her face. She looked older this way. More confident, too.

At the Academy, Janine had fit in better than Annabelle did in some ways, since she was smart. But Gray Island wasn't exactly a diverse place. There were some other black kids who boarded at the Academy, but not many. And there were even fewer black families who lived on the island. More came from the mainland for vacation . . . but not *that* many more.

Annabelle wondered what it had been like for Janine

to stand out from other island kids in *two* ways—because she went to the Academy *and* because her skin was a different color—and what a relief it must have been to go to college in New York City, where she probably didn't have to stand out so much all the time.

"You ready to start?" Janine asked.

They took turns reading pages aloud, and Janine paused to ask comprehension questions all the time because even though Annabelle's "verbal intelligence" and "reading fluency" were technically sort of high according to all that testing she'd had, her "processing ability" was terrible, which meant she had trouble remembering what she'd read. And when Annabelle couldn't answer Janine's comprehension questions because she'd zoned out staring at the sparkling gray ocean and wondering if the team would win their meet on the Cape today without her, they had to go back and read the last page all over again.

After they'd finally finished a chapter, Janine nodded at someone at the other end of the room, over by the copier. It was a shortish guy who was wearing khaki shorts that ended halfway down his calves and waving at Janine with a grin on his face. Annabelle didn't know his name, but she knew he was in Connor's class at Gray Island High. She'd seen them hanging out together in town.

"My friend's little brother," Janine said. "I saw him at a party last weekend. I remember him being, like, *your* age."

The way she said it made it sound like somebody Annabelle's age would still ride a bike with training wheels.

The guy headed over.

"How's it going, Mark?" Janine said.

"Hey! You coming tomorrow night?" he asked. "Bonfire on the beach by Bailey Sound. Should be a good crowd."

He stuck his hands into the pockets of his too-long shorts and leaned back a little, puffing out his chest. There was something too purposeful about the way he stood there—like he was telling himself to be casual. Annabelle thought of math problems and how you were always supposed to show your work so the teacher would know what you were trying to do. In real life, it was better if people *couldn't* see so clearly what you were attempting.

"I don't think so," Janine said. "But have fun."

"Next time, maybe?" the guy—Mark—asked.

Janine gave him the same vague, let's-keep-things-moving nod Annabelle got when she tried to talk about something other than her work.

"Sure, maybe."

Then Mark trudged away, and Janine searched the book for the place they'd left off. Did Janine not realize that this guy liked her? Or not really care, since she was in college and he was still in high school?

"Okay, you're three-quarters of the way down this page," Janine said.

Annabelle found the spot and began to read again, but then she glanced up, out the window at that distant line of ocean, and something occurred to her.

Good crowd, Mark had said when he was trying to convince Janine about the party.

Mark was Connor's friend, and if there really was a good crowd at this bonfire, then probably Connor would be there, too. And maybe when Annabelle and Connor texted next, he'd invite her to come along. She got excited for a second before she remembered Mom and Mitch were barely letting her leave the house. There was no way she'd be allowed to go even if he did.

The next day, Annabelle was lounging in front of the TV when her phone buzzed with a text. She lunged across the couch for it hoping maybe it was Connor, but it was Elisa instead.

Hey Annabelle, Elisa had written. **Kayla's coming over tonight for pizza and movies. You should come too!**

Annabelle smiled as she read the words. Elisa and

Kayla didn't have to be nice to her when she wasn't even swimming with them anymore, but they actually wanted to hang out with her. And then her smile grew as she read Elisa's next text, with her address.

In Bailey Sound. Where there was going to be a bonfire that Connor would almost definitely be at. That maybe Elisa and Kayla would want to go to, if Annabelle could only get permission to be at Elisa's house.

Chapter 24

Mom was working an afternoon wedding, and it took about two seconds for Annabelle to convince Mitch she should be allowed to go to Elisa's. He called Mom's cell and somehow convinced her, too.

"We both think it's good for you to have some time with nice friends," he told Annabelle.

Annabelle knew how Mitch's brain worked, so she was pretty sure she knew what else he was thinking. Maybe if she developed some good, wholesome friendships with girls like Elisa, who had pizza-and-movie nights instead of sneaking off to meet Connor Madison and sprain their wrists and fracture their thumb bones, Mom would think going back to the high school team was good for her after all, once she finally recovered. Maybe she could get back by the end of the season, before the South Shore rematch.

Mitch tried to make conversation on the way to Elisa's, asking about how Annabelle's wrist was feeling and whether she wanted to make s'mores at the little beach tomorrow night, and whether she thought his daughters might like a snorkeling trip out on Jeremy's dad's boat when they visited in August. It all felt pretty forced, though, so after a while, Annabelle turned up the radio and zoned out, trying to remember what it had been like to sit in her dad's car when *he* drove her places when she was a kid.

She wondered if he still had the same car he'd had when she was little, that black Honda. If he still listened to sports radio and liked rolling down the windows instead of using the air-conditioning, even on the highway.

He must have gotten her letter by now, and she imagined him first seeing her handwriting, which was smaller and more mature than it had been when she'd last written him a card. She wondered if he'd been surprised to hear from her, since it had taken her so long to write. If maybe he'd started to believe she wouldn't.

"Well, here we are," Mitch said when they pulled up in front of Elisa's house.

They did the usual kiss and catch, and he waited in the driveway until Elisa's mom opened the front door and waved to him.

In the kitchen, Elisa and Kayla were rolling out pizza dough.

"I'm so glad you could come!" Elisa said, giving Annabelle a hug.

Kayla hugged her, too, and Annabelle wondered how much Jeremy had told her about what had happened that night, from his warped Annabelle-and-Connor-are-both-awful perspective. She wondered how much Elisa knew, too, since Elisa hadn't even been there.

Elisa and Kayla both wore tank tops and jean shorts, and Annabelle felt out of place. She'd tried on lots of different outfits in case they really did go to the bonfire and had finally decided on the white denim capris Mia had said made her butt look good back when Mia still gave her compliments. She'd paired them with Mom's long-sleeved, wide-necked, blue-and-white-striped shirt. She was ten times dressier than Kayla and Elisa, and she'd probably just get pizza sauce on her white pants.

"I feel so bad that you fell," Kayla said, touching Annabelle's wrist brace. "I knew that whole thing was a terrible idea. I should have said something."

"I'm sorry I wasn't there," Elisa added, glancing at Kayla. "I . . . had plans with some other friends, but . . . I didn't realize it would be like that."

"It's fine," Annabelle said, straightening the bottom of her too-fancy shirt and swallowing the words she wanted to say: *I can make my own decisions*, and *I can take care of myself!*

Yes, everything had turned out pretty terribly, but that was bad luck. That didn't mean she'd needed Kayla to send her and Jeremy home like little kids with an early bedtime or Elisa to somehow intervene.

"It's really so bad that you can't swim the whole rest of the summer?" Kayla asked.

"Well . . . it'll be a while," Annabelle said, messing with the fraying Velcro on the brace.

There was a long pause before Elisa announced, "The dough's all ready! Let's make some pizza!"

So they made one pepperoni and one with lots of veggies, and then Elisa insisted on a weird one with random stuff from the fridge and cabinets. She used pesto instead of tomato sauce and layered artichoke hearts and banana peppers on top of the cheese. Kayla had to stop her from adding canned pineapple, too.

"It's Hawaiian!" Elisa said.

"Um, not with pesto and this other stuff," Kayla told her.

But they were all laughing and having fun now. Elisa was good at realizing when people were uncomfortable and doing something to break the tension.

And actually, the weird pizza wasn't bad. Kayla stuck to the veggie kind, and Annabelle caught herself doing what Jeremy would have done if he was here—noticing what food Kayla chose and how long it took her to eat it—but she told herself to stop. That was kind of like Mia watching when Annabelle got a test back to see whether or not she was upset. It felt terrible to know that other people were too aware of something that made you vulnerable. She knew that firsthand.

Nobody said anything else about swim team or the night at Dennis Martin's house. They debated which island pizza place was the best and talked about how much money you could make babysitting for summer families, and then Kayla asked about a guy Elisa liked at Beach Buzz.

Annabelle got a jolt of extra energy, as if she'd finished the entire bottle of Dr. Pepper Elisa had set out and not just one cup's worth.

If the conversation was turning to crushes, maybe they'd ask her if there was anybody *she* was into. Maybe they'd specifically ask her about Connor, even. Maybe there would be a good time to bring up going to the bonfire.

"We've been texting a little," Elisa said, and Kayla set down the piece of pizza she was eating as if this conversation required her full attention.

"Who usually texts first, you or him?" she asked. "And how often?"

Elisa laughed. "Um, him mostly I guess? And most days we end up texting. But I text with you most days, too. It might not mean anything."

"Yeah, but it's different when it's a guy, right?" Annabelle asked, and Kayla and Elisa both looked at her.

Maybe that had been a little too quick, the way she'd jumped in there. Maybe she'd sounded a little too desperate for them to agree.

"I don't know," Elisa said slowly. "I have guy friends I text a lot with, too. This feels different, but it's hard to be sure. He's not a super-flirty guy, though, I don't think. So that makes it seem like it could be more."

She shrugged and helped herself to another piece of the weird pizza. And then she and Kayla locked eyes for way too long.

"Well, that's good," Kayla said, but her voice was stiff, as if she were reciting lines she'd memorized for a play. "There are some people who are so super flirtatious that it's hard to tell what it means when they pay lots of attention to you."

"Yeah," Elisa agreed. "My friend Lucy's like that. She's really affectionate, and she's definitely confused people before." She paused and picked up a banana pepper that had fallen off her slice of pizza. "Connor's like that, too."

And now Elisa and Kayla were both watching Annabelle. That jolt she'd felt moments before tipped from excited to panicked. What was happening here?

Kayla nodded. "Right. He's cute and all, obviously. But *such* a flirt."

The windows a few feet away from Elisa's kitchen table were open, letting in the cool ocean air, but Annabelle's skin burned so hot that she pushed up her sleeves and fanned her face with her hand.

Why were they saying this? Yes, Connor put his arm around lots of people and chatted with everybody. But he wasn't *just* flirting with *her*. Was he?

"We . . . noticed he's been paying a lot of attention to you," Elisa said to Annabelle, and for a second Annabelle was happy, just as she had been when Mitch had noticed the same thing. But then Elisa added, "And Kayla told me a little about the night you got hurt. And . . . he's a lot older than you are, you know?"

Annabelle wanted to scream.

"He's not *that* much older than me," she squeaked out. "Two years is *nothing*."

"It's kind of *not* nothing when it's the difference between middle school and high school, though," Kayla said quietly.

And now Annabelle was thinking of what Mitch had said the other morning when he and Mom got so mad. How no high school boy should be paying this kind of attention to her. How she was a *kid*. But that was wrong. She'd thought Kayla and Elisa would understand even though Mitch didn't.

But they were in high school, too. They were a year older than Connor, even. Had they only invited her here tonight for some big-sister intervention, not because they were actually her friends?

And what right did they have to do that? What did they actually know? Kayla hadn't ever dated anybody, as far as Annabelle knew. And it's not like they'd watched every interaction Annabelle and Connor had ever had or read every text.

"You know what?" Elisa said. "I think we need chocolate for this conversation! Who wants brownies?"

But there was no way brownies were going to break all *this* tension.

"I'm—I'm actually going to use the bathroom," Annabelle stammered.

When she closed the door behind her, she tried to think of an excuse to leave. She could say she didn't feel well. Call Mitch to come pick her up. She pulled her phone out of her back pocket and gasped. There was a text from Connor.

What's up HB? he'd written.

Connor had texted her first! At six, right after Mitch had dropped her off. And on a Saturday night! This was proof that Kayla and Elisa didn't understand.

Not much, she typed back with shaking thumbs. **What are you up to?**

Then she stared at the screen.

Come on, come on, come on!

Ugh, why hadn't she checked her phone earlier, so she could have written back when he was still paying attention? He might have been texting to invite her to the bonfire!

Actually, he *must* have been texting to invite her. She and Connor didn't usually text until eight or nine at night. The only other time he'd texted in the early evening was when he was telling her everyone was going to the Creamery.

And the party was *right* there down the road. So close she was surprised they couldn't hear it through the open windows.

She put her phone away and went back out to the kitchen.

"Um, I actually have to go," she said. "My mom's home and she's all mad that Mitch let me come when we were supposed to have family time."

Elisa frowned. "You have to go *now*?"

"Yep!" Annabelle gave a little shrug, like, *What can*

you do? You know moms. "Mitch is on his way, I guess. I'm supposed to wait outside."

She wasn't sure they believed her, but she also wasn't sure she really cared. Not when Connor was so close by.

"We didn't mean to upset you," Kayla said.

"I know Connor pretty well," Elisa added. "He's the kind of guy who wants every pretty girl he meets to think he's amazing and pay lots of attention to him. Every *person* he meets, really."

"We don't want someone like Connor to make you feel bad," Kayla said.

So *they* had decided to gang up on her and make her feel bad instead? And what was that supposed to mean, "someone like Connor"? How well could Elisa possibly know him? They barely hung out at swim team stuff at all. She hadn't even been there that night at the Creamery when the rest of the group was hanging out.

"I really have to go," Annabelle lied. She didn't even put her plate in the sink and rinse it. Her mom would be horrified, but whatever. Kayla and Elisa *deserved* to have to wash her plate. "Thanks for the pizza and everything!" she said. "See you soon!"

Except she wouldn't, really. She wasn't going back to the team, and she wasn't going to accept any more girls' night invitations after today. And that was fine by her.

Chapter 25

As Annabelle walked to the beach entrance at the end of the street, the sounds of music and laughter floated toward her.

The bonfire was going strong, but the wind had picked up and Annabelle shivered. People here weren't as dressed up as she was, either. Most of the girls had on sweatshirts or fleeces with jeans. Before she spotted anybody she recognized, she saw the beer cans glinting in the fire's orange glow.

Of course there was beer. It was a high school party. She thought about leaving and calling Mitch for real, but then she spotted Connor.

He was sitting in the sand with his legs bent toward him and his elbows resting on his knees. He had on a baseball cap—that's why she hadn't found him right away. She'd been searching for his blond hair, which barely peeked out in the back, curling a tiny bit at the ends. Jordan was next to him, holding a beer, and Mark from the library was on Jordan's other side with a shiny blue can propped up in the sand next to him. But Connor didn't have one.

Connor wasn't with Ruby, *and* he wasn't drinking. The dread that had sunk to the bottom of Annabelle's stomach in a tight wad when she saw the beer cans began to loosen, like the saltwater taffy she and Mia used to buy in town and pull apart into thin, stringy bites.

"Annabelle!" Ruby's voice. Great. She was with a girl Annabelle recognized from the Academy. Genevieve, another day student, who played lacrosse with Mia and had just finished eighth grade.

"What's up?" Ruby asked, her skinny eyebrows raised into arches. "What are you doing here?"

Annabelle launched into a too-long explanation about how Mitch was running late to pick her up from Elisa's, and she'd heard the party while she was waiting and wandered down.

"Um, this might not be your kind of thing," Ruby said.

Right. Because Ruby thought Annabelle was such a baby. Genevieve hadn't started high school yet, either. Why was this party okay for Genevieve and not okay for Annabelle?

Annabelle flexed the fingers on her sore hand and changed the subject. "Sorry you have to do the fly leg now for the relay."

Ruby shrugged. "We were way better with me swimming breast and you on fly. But we'll be okay most meets even if we don't win the medley. Just heal well and all. There's always next summer, right?"

Annabelle nodded. "Okay, yeah. Well, see you later."

She took off toward Connor as fast as her feet could move in the thick, cool sand, so she wouldn't lose her nerve.

"So who else is coming Monday?" Mark was asking Jordan. "You gonna ask that swim team girl? Rachel or whatever?"

There wasn't a Rachel on the team. Ruby?

"Maybe. How many extra tickets do we have?" Jordan asked.

"Two, if your sister's coming," Mark said. "It's the three of us plus Natalie and Liz."

Annabelle stood a few feet away, not sure how to let them know she was there. She racked her brain for something going on on Monday, but she had no idea.

Then Jordan saw her. "Oh. Hi."

No name, like maybe he couldn't even place her.

And now Connor noticed her, too. She waited for that look to cross his face. That laser-focused, no-one-else-I'd-rather-see look.

But it was different, the way his eyes widened and his eyebrows went up this time. He was surprised to see her, which made sense. But was he more confused-surprised than happy-surprised?

That taffy clump of dread hardened in her stomach.

"Hey there, Hummingbird," he said.

"You're the girl from the library, right?" Mark asked. "With Janine?"

Annabelle nodded. "Yeah. Hey."

"Maybe Janine wants to come to the concert," Jordan said, elbowing Mark and laughing his squawking seagull laugh.

There was an indent in the sand next to Connor, like somebody had just been sitting there before getting up to join a different conversation. Annabelle plopped down into it. "What concert?" she asked.

"It's in Boston," Mark said. The way he said it made it clear that he assumed she'd never be interesting or mature enough to go to a concert in Boston, and now she didn't feel bad for him anymore about Janine blowing him off.

"The band's called Level Up," Connor added. "They're playing at Brighton Music Hall."

Annabelle had never heard of the band or the place where they were playing, but she nodded anyway. "Nice."

Mark picked up his beer and Jordan did the same, as if the impulse to take a sip was contagious, like yawning.

Annabelle was grateful Connor didn't have one. Mitch and Mom had wine or beer at dinner sometimes, and that was fine. But she'd never been able to forget the way her dad had slurred late at night or the way he swayed and couldn't focus his eyes on her that terrible day when he showed up drunk at swim practice. She knew he was better now, but still. She didn't want to think about Connor acting anything like that.

Connor glanced over at Mark, and she couldn't read the look that passed between them. She bent her knees to her chest and brushed sand off the calves of her white jeans, which were all wrong for a party like this.

"So, HB," Connor started. "There's something I should maybe . . . tell you real quick."

Annabelle planted her good hand in the sand and burrowed her fingers in. Those words could be good—some kind of confession about how he felt. But would he do that right in front of Jordan and Mark? And would that be quick?

She slid her fingers under the surface of the sand until she found a rock, and then she closed her hand around it and squeezed.

And that's when the girl showed up. Wavy brown hair that flew around her face in the wind, rosy cheeks, and eyes that could have been pale brown or pale green or hazel—Annabelle couldn't see well enough in the twilight to be sure. The girl carried a shiny blue beer can in each hand, and the pieces started to shift together, even though they still didn't quite click. The indent in the sand right next to Connor. No beer for Connor when Annabelle sat, but an extra one in this girl's hand.

Connor cleared his throat and rubbed one hand around in the sand, leaving a ripply arch shape.

"Hi there," the girl said.

Her cheeks were seriously rosy. As if she'd been out shoveling in a snowstorm instead of hanging out at a beach party. They made her look pretty in a low-key, outdoorsy kind of way.

"Who's your friend, Con?"

Con. And now Annabelle saw the way she looked at him. Tilted head. Small, private smile. Like he was *hers*. And her eyes were hazel—Annabelle could tell for sure now.

Annabelle felt like she'd been underwater too long, and she was struggling to make it up for air.

"Caroline, this is Annabelle," Connor mumbled, and *his* face was pink, too. Not rosy-cheeked like this Caroline. Embarrassed.

Was he embarrassed for *Annabelle*?

Did he know why she was really here at the party?

Why she texted him all the time, thinking—*ack!*—thinking she was being confident and spontaneous, not pathetic and desperate?

He knew she liked him, so he'd been about to tell her about *Caroline*. To break it to her that he was taken.

And now Annabelle was in Caroline's seat. She'd been getting herself all worked up over every message from Connor, convincing herself that every reply was proof of his interest. She'd thought Kayla and Elisa didn't know what they were talking about. She'd thought Ruby was her biggest competition. She never in a million years would have believed that there could be someone else completely.

"I like your shirt," Caroline said. "It's adorable."

Adorable. Like a puppy or a baby or a personalized purple towel.

A few hours before, Annabelle had admired the way the thin striped fabric clung to her chest and waist. But now she saw: It didn't matter that the shirt showed off her new curves. She only looked like she was trying too hard—playing dress-up in her mom's clothes.

"I—I'd better go," Annabelle stammered. "I was just coming for a little walk while I was waiting for my ride."

"Have a good night," Connor said.

As if that was possible now. And as soon as she got up, he reached for the beer can Caroline held out to him and swallowed down a gulp.

On her way back to the dunes, Annabelle had to pass a cluster of girls. Ruby. Genevieve. A couple of other summer girls she didn't know.

Annabelle wished Mia were there. The old Mia, who would link arms with her and pull her into that cluster where she could just be one girl in a group. No more obvious than anyone else.

"Hey, Annabelle," Ruby called.

Her voice was kind. Like maybe she'd been upset to see that Connor had a girlfriend, too, so she knew how Annabelle felt? Or maybe *she'd* known better, but she felt sorry for poor innocent, little-girl Annabelle?

Either way, that kindness pulled tears into the corners of Annabelle's eyes.

"I'll see you later," she said, rushing away from Ruby and the other girls, toward the beach exit.

When she looked back one last time, Caroline was back in her seat in the sand, and her head rested on Connor's shoulder.

No swimming, no Mia, no Jeremy, and now no Connor. And Annabelle was as clueless with boys as she was with everything else. She couldn't read a guy like Connor any better than she could read her history textbook.

Chapter 26

When Annabelle finally made it home, she heard Mom and Mitch out on the deck, laughing.

"And then the oysters started to come out completely frozen—hard as rocks—when the whole reason they wanted the wedding at the Charthouse was the promise of fresh fish!" Mom was saying.

"What did you do?" Mitch asked.

"Told the servers to take those oysters right back to the kitchen and top off everybody's wineglasses to keep them happy while they waited for food. Then I told the grooms that serving a light fish course *after* the entrées was more cosmopolitan, and I told the kitchen they had thirty minutes to figure out how to thaw the oysters or else I'd tell every couple I meet with that their fish isn't so fresh after all. I made sure those oysters came off the bill, too."

Mitch chuckled. "You're a genius."

Mom the genius and Mitch the strategizer, problem-solving their way to success.

Mom had been successful way before they moved to Gray Island and she started her event-planning business—she'd gotten lots of promotions at her old PR firm. One time, at a party for Mom's old job, Annabelle had overheard a man with a bushy mustache saying that if Mom hadn't gone part-time for a while when Annabelle was really little, she'd be running the whole department.

And Mitch had been profiled in a magazine piece about Gray Island "movers and shakers" last year—there was a whole article with pictures and everything about how he'd left his New York City finance job and built up his financial planning office here because he saw a need on the island and had the guts to take a chance.

"Belle?" Mom called, and Annabelle slid open the screen door to join them on the deck.

They were sitting at the table, with Mom's feet on Mitch's lap and a glass of wine in front of each of them.

"How'd you get home?" Mitch asked. "I would have come to get you."

"Got a ride," Annabelle mumbled. She didn't add that

the ride came from the bus driver, or that she'd had to wait twenty-five minutes for the bus and trek home from the closest stop, almost a mile away.

"That shirt's so cute on you," Mom said. "I'm glad you had a night with friends, honey. Did you have fun with the girls?"

She sounded so hopeful. So eager to know that Annabelle wasn't a complete disaster—that at least she could handle making some nice friends and spending a pleasant evening with them.

"Sit down and join us," Mitch offered.

But Annabelle's clothes smelled like the bonfire, and anyway, Mom and Mitch were so happy there, just the two of them.

On the floor of the deck, those newer planks of wood were *still* the littlest bit lighter and smoother than the old ones. When they'd set up the deck furniture in the spring, she'd caught Mom sighing over them.

Mom leaned forward, squinting to see Annabelle better. "Are you okay? Did something happen?"

"My hand's just bothering me. I'm gonna go ice it before bed."

She went up to her room even though it was barely nine and checked her phone as a reflex, as if there might be a message from Connor. And then a giant wave of humiliation threatened to drag her under and spin her dizzy as she looked at the blank display.

Connor had never been interested in her. He flirted with everybody, like Elisa and Kayla had said. He'd probably only kept their text conversations going because he was bored.

Annabelle didn't have any new text messages—no surprise there. But she *did* have new messages in her email. She tapped on her inbox and then gasped.

She'd given him her email address in her letter, and he'd written.

Her dad had written her back.

Her letter had made his day, that's what the email said. He said he was *thrilled* to hear from her. He said they could email back and forth to get to know each other again, if that's what she was comfortable with. He'd wait until she was ready to talk on the phone, and he wouldn't push for a visit yet. But whenever she was ready, she was welcome.

He didn't say a whole lot about himself—only that he was working at a coffee shop for now, right down the street from his apartment. "Nothing too fancy," he wrote. "But I get to come up with new menu items. I added that grilled cheese you used to love, with goat cheese and strawberries."

She remembered that sandwich, with little green basil leaves peeking out. "Grown-up grilled cheese," Dad had called it. She'd felt so sophisticated when she ate it.

It was true that his new job didn't sound as impressive as Mitch's or Mom's. But it sounded a lot better than what he used to do, trying to sell real estate when nobody seemed to be buying houses. Or at least, no one seemed to be buying houses from him.

Then he asked question after question. About which events she was swimming and who her friends were and what the best part was about summer in Gray Island. Ten questions in a row—like there were so many things he wanted to know—and not a single one about how she was doing in school.

She started to write back immediately, but it would take a long time to reply to all those questions in just the right way. She stopped partway through, leaving the rest to come back to later.

It was the first time she could ever remember leaving questions until the next day because she was looking forward to finishing them and didn't want to rush, not because she got too discouraged and had no idea what to say.

Chapter 27

That night, as Annabelle lay there in bed picturing Caroline snuggled up next to Connor, she almost convinced herself she could leave Gray Island and go live with her dad.

The shame she felt over Connor—it was big. Really, really big. But it probably wasn't anywhere near as big as the shame Dad had felt that day when her old coach had sent him home from swim practice. If her shame was as long as the marsh that stretched along the bottom part of the island, his was probably ocean-sized.

He was proof that people messed up sometimes and could bounce back and be okay. That not everybody did the right thing all the time. Maybe he would understand her in a way Mom and Mitch didn't.

But then the next morning, Mitch knocked on her door. "Waffles or pancakes?" he asked, as if that were even a question. And she couldn't imagine *not* living with him, even though things had been weird.

Waffles were still her favorite, just like they had been the day she and Mitch had first met and he'd made her a whipped cream smiley face. As the first batch filled the kitchen with their sweet, warm smell, she breathed it in and tried to calm down.

Maybe last night hadn't been quite as humiliating as she'd thought. Maybe Ruby and Genevieve and those other girls didn't actually realize what had happened with her and Connor. And maybe Connor didn't actually realize she liked him. Maybe he'd been about to tell her something else. About swim team or something.

Maybe it wasn't quite as obvious as she'd feared, how badly she fit here. Only Mom noticed the barely different wood beams on the deck. Maybe only Annabelle knew what a mess she'd made of everything.

When Mitch dropped her off for her first physical therapy session the next morning, things felt almost normal between them.

"Do good work in there, kiddo. That's one important arm you have," he said, and then he blew her a kiss and drove off to his office, a few blocks off the main street.

The physical therapist's office was next to Beach Buzz Coffee. After her session, she was supposed to hang out at Beach Buzz until it was time for tutoring, and she was really, really hoping Elisa wasn't working this morning. Not after the other night.

Mitch had let her off right in front of the little market on the corner, where Mrs. Green sometimes sent her and Jeremy to get a lemon or an onion or something else she needed for dinner. Annabelle felt a pang of sadness as she thought of Jeremy, off in Boston and still mad at her. She wished she could send him a talking-animal video and make everything between them okay.

Could she, maybe? Jeremy wasn't usually the kind of person to stay mad. He wasn't like Mia, who could—

Mia.

There she was, halfway down the block, between Annabelle and the physical therapist's office. She was holding some kind of iced drink from Beach Buzz and walking with two other girls. One was tiny, with bright blond hair that had pale purple streaks in the front. Reagan.

So she had come to visit, like Mia had wanted. And the other was tall, dark-haired Genevieve, from the bonfire.

"Oh, look who it is!" Reagan said. "Hey, Annabelle! Genevieve was just telling us she saw you Saturday night."

Reagan said it like it was some big happy coincidence. One of her loud, look-at-me laughs bubbled up behind her loud, look-at-me voice.

Genevieve messed with the straw in her drink. She glanced down at the sidewalk, then up at the sky, then across the street at the preppy store where summer people shopped: everywhere except at Annabelle.

So Genevieve knew, then. She and Ruby and all of those other girls knew that Annabelle had practically thrown herself at Connor when Connor had been there with his *girlfriend*! And now she felt guilty because she'd told gossipy Reagan, who thought the whole thing was funny.

And even worse, she'd told Mia.

"So Connor has a girlfriend, huh?" Mia said. "*That* must have been rough to find out."

Her voice wasn't all-out gleeful like Reagan's, but it wasn't sympathetic, either. It was sort of . . . satisfied. Like Annabelle had gotten what she deserved. Before, Annabelle had thought there was nothing worse than when Mia got all "poor Annabelle" pitying, but this right now was worse.

Mia was *glad* that Connor had a girlfriend.

She was glad that Annabelle wouldn't ever catch up in the ongoing competition their friendship had become. This was how terrible things had gotten between them: Something bad had happened to Annabelle, and Mia wasn't even sorry.

And now she and Reagan and Genevieve would go on with their fun summer day as soon as they said good-bye to Annabelle. Every once in a while, Mia might say something about how ridiculous Annabelle had been to think she had a shot with Connor. Or how happy she was that she'd made friends who weren't so clueless. But otherwise, they'd do whatever they'd planned—go to the beach, maybe, and the Creamery. Or to play mini golf, except making up silly rules would probably be way too immature for the *new* Mia, so they'd play the normal way and take selfies at every hole to post on social media so everyone would know how much fun they were having.

But *Annabelle* couldn't have a normal day. Not when everyone knew she'd thought Connor liked her but he didn't. Not when everyone would pity her even more than they did at school when a teacher made her answer a question in front of the whole class and she got it wrong, again.

She needed to get away from Mia.

She needed to get away from the feeling that she was doing every single thing wrong and everybody knew it.

But how could she get away from that feeling when she couldn't get away from *herself*?

"I—I have to go," she said, bolting down the sidewalk, right past the physical therapist's office where she was supposed to go inside.

She kept on going past Beach Buzz, and when she peeked in, she saw Elisa at the counter. Did Elisa already know what had happened, too? How Annabelle had lied and ditched her and Kayla for the party, where Connor had only proven them right?

At the next corner, a taxi pulled up to the curb and a family of summer people tumbled out.

Annabelle had her wallet in her bag with $60 from Mom to pay Janine, plus $10 from Mitch to get a snack after physical therapy and $14 left over from the last time she babysat the Bennett girls. Eighty-four dollars had to be plenty.

"Taxi!" she called. "Wait, please!"

She couldn't believe the cabdriver actually stopped.

She slid into the back seat of the cab, and the driver said, "Where to, miss?"

He probably figured she was a summer person. Only summer people took taxis. She wished she *were* a summer person. Or anybody other than herself.

"Miss?" the driver said, turning his head around. "Where are you heading?"

He was wearing a Red Sox cap, and she decided to take that as a sign.

She couldn't escape herself, but she *could* escape this tiny island where she couldn't even walk down one block on Main Street without running into people she didn't want to see. At least for the day, anyway, and that was something.

"The ferry, please," she said.

And off they went, bumping over cobblestones as the cab headed down the hill toward the harbor.

Chapter 28

The first time Annabelle had taken the ferry back to the mainland, she, Mom, and Mitch had gone straight up to the open-air top deck. There, they'd watched the island get smaller and smaller until it disappeared, and then they'd looked out at the steel-blue open ocean as the ferry glided along.

These days, whether she was with Mom and Mitch or Mia's family, they usually found an open table on the enclosed second deck, since the view was nothing new. But today she followed the summer people to the top, where the salty wind whipped the front pieces of her hair loose from her ponytail and made the corners of her eyes water.

When the ferry looped out from the harbor toward the open ocean, a mom led her two sunburned kids up to the railing.

"Look straight at the lighthouse and make a wish to come back next summer!" she told them.

Annabelle knew about the Bruck Point Lighthouse wish tradition. People used to throw pennies into the water for good luck, to make sure they'd return. Over the years, the penny part had stopped because it wasn't good for the fish or seagulls, but people had kept up the wishing.

Annabelle looked out at the open ocean instead of back at the black-and-white lighthouse. Whitecaps crashed against the sides of the ferry, but it slid along, too big to be shaken by even the biggest waves. Ahead of her, Cape Cod was there in the distance, past the edge of what she could see. That's where she'd get the bus that would take her to Boston.

For today, it was better to focus her eyes forward, even without a point to wish on, than to look back toward home.

The round-trip bus fare from the ferry terminal into Boston was $36 because she was too old for the child rate she and Mia had gotten last summer. She'd already spent $4 on the cab and $40 on her round-trip ferry ticket, and she needed $2.20 for a student CharlieCard to take two trips on the T.

That meant she'd have only $1.80 of her $84 left over.

She sucked it up and handed over the money. It was okay, she told herself. All she really needed to spend money on was transportation. Dad worked at a coffee shop, after all. He'd give her food when she got there. One of his special strawberry grilled cheese sandwiches.

She checked the time on her phone as she sat down to wait for the bus. Ten minutes until her tutoring session with Janine.

Janine was going to text Mom when she didn't show up, and then Mom would call Annabelle right away. She was lucky the physical therapist hadn't called Mitch already—or that Mitch was busy and hadn't taken the call.

She used her phone to look up how to take the T to the address on Dad's envelope. He'd said the coffee shop was down the street from where he lived, and she figured that's where he'd be. She wrote the directions on the back of her ferry ticket and then sent a quick text to both Mom and Mitch.

I'm going to Boston for the day. I'm sorry. I'm fine and will see you tonight. Love you.

She thought about adding, *Please don't worry*, but she knew that was pointless. So she just turned off her phone so she wouldn't have to read their frantic messages and they couldn't track where she was and show up at Dad's coffee shop to drag her home.

On the bus, Annabelle tried to call up some good memories of her dad. She grabbed onto a few: Dad staying home with her when she was sick, bringing her applesauce and cinnamon toast and watching game shows with her on TV. That swim out to the buoy the summer they went to the Jersey Shore. Dad carrying her around on his shoulders at the Labor Day parade so she could see and riding the teacups with her over and over at the carnival afterward.

But then she remembered the rest of that Labor Day. It was after he'd lost his real estate job. Mom had gone in to work—she had to work even more once Dad didn't anymore—but Dad was supposed to take Annabelle to the parade and the carnival.

Annabelle had gotten dressed in the pink polka-dotted tank top and blue shorts Mom had laid out for her, and she'd waited outside Dad's room, softly knocking every so often, until he finally got out of bed.

He had to carry her on his shoulders because they were so late that they were stuck at the back of the crowd, and they only saw the last few floats. They missed the high school soccer team's float, and that was the part she'd been most excited about. Her favorite babysitter was the goalie, and she'd promised to save watermelon Jolly Ranchers to throw to Annabelle as she passed by.

Dad let Annabelle ride the teacups for ages to make up for missing so much of the parade, and then he bought her so much funnel cake and cotton candy that she threw up on the way back to the car.

She grasped for more good memories, but the good ones were like fine grains of sand, sliding right through her fingers even when she closed her hand. And now the worst one came back, from that swim team practice in fourth grade, and she couldn't fight off the thought she usually managed to block out.

That her dad was supposed to protect her—that's what dads *did*—but he'd been about to put her in danger that day. It was her coach who had protected her, and then Mom and Mitch. Not Dad.

But that was a long time ago. Things were different now.

The bus wound through neighborhoods and then past gas stations and strip malls, and she thought of Jeremy taking this same drive to Boston a few days before, watching this same scenery pass by and still being mad at her. It was silly to think she could make anything better just by sending him a video to make him laugh.

But then she remembered: Connor was going to make the trip, too. Today.

That's what Jordan had said at the party, before . . . everything with Caroline. Probably not this early, since they were going to a concert at night. But maybe Annabelle would take the T back to the bus station in Boston right when Connor and Jordan's bus was getting in. She imagined Connor's grin widening as he saw her.

"Hummingbird!" he would call.

And she'd be hesitant at first, after Saturday night. But Connor would leave the others and walk over to her. He'd put his hands on her arms like he had when she'd stumbled into him at the pool the day Colette had asked her to swim up with the high school team. And he'd tell her how sorry he was that he hadn't told her about Caroline. How he and Caroline had been together for a long time, and he didn't want to hurt her, but he couldn't help the way he felt about Annabelle.

That happened sometimes. Mia's cousin—the same one who had told them about how liking somebody is like looking at them through 3-D glasses when the rest of the world is in blurry 2-D—had been dating someone else when she'd started hanging out with the boyfriend she was always texting with. But it turned out she liked the new guy even more.

Annabelle rested her own hands on her upper arms, where she imagined Connor placing his, and she rubbed them up and down as she shivered in the bus's blasting air-conditioning.

It was dangerous, letting herself imagine this when she'd already felt the icy-sharp stab of finding out Connor was with Caroline. It was like getting into the water on a too-cold day. It was never comfortable, but the initial shock was the worst part, and if you got out and then had to get back in, you felt it all over again. But she couldn't help herself.

By the time Annabelle got on the T, her stomach was growling. She hadn't eaten in ages.

What if her dad wasn't working today and wasn't at his apartment? Would someone else at his coffee shop give her food if she said they were related?

A guy wearing a Patriots T-shirt wanted to sit down next to her, so Annabelle had to pick her bag up off the seat for him. When she lifted it, she felt something hard in the outer pocket.

The rock she'd picked up the night of the bonfire,

when she'd burrowed her hand in the sand as she waited to hear what Connor was going to tell her. She'd held on to it without realizing and slipped it into the pocket of her bag on the bus ride home that night.

It was a salt-and-pepper granite. Not as pretty as pink or white quartz. Not even white and black like salt and pepper, really. Just light gray with darker gray speckles. It was sort of an oval, but with one fat end and one skinny one, and the skinny end had a pointy bump. She gripped the rock in her good hand and rubbed her fingertip over the point.

She tried again with the happy memories. Dad made the best mac and cheese, and he'd made it week after week if she asked for it. He laughed as hard as she did at the cartoons they watched on the weekends, and he taught her how to ride a bike when she was six. And . . . she couldn't remember much else. It was Mitch who ruffled the top of her hair and made waffles on weekends and cheered the loudest at her swim meets. She kept trying to call up a memory of Dad and getting one of Mitch instead.

But she'd been living with Mitch for years now, so no wonder she had fresher memories with him. That didn't mean anything, really. She could make all sorts of new ones with Dad now. In her head, she recited all those questions from his email, the ones she hadn't finished typing out answers to but could answer in person instead.

The train approached his stop, and she took her three deep breaths.

She could start making new memories right now.

Chapter 29

Dad's address wasn't too far from the T stop where Annabelle got off. The neighborhood was sort of in the city but sort of not. Over her head, tall trees stretched their green branches over the sidewalk, shading her from the afternoon sun. Old houses—some in good shape and some with peeling paint and dried-out brown plants in window boxes—sat right smack next to each other, sharing walls. Every once in a while, a little store or restaurant interrupted the row of homes.

Pretty soon, she saw it. Beans and Books Café and Bookshop.

Bookshop?

Dad, who had stood up for her when Mom was always nagging her about reading, was working at a coffee shop that sold *books*?

The bells on the door jangled way too loudly as Annabelle went inside, and the thick, slightly sharp smell of coffee hit her. The coffee shop part was to the left—a long counter with a chalkboard menu hanging on the wall, a glass display of baked goods, and ten or twelve little tables. Then to the right was the bookstore. You had to go up two stairs, and a chalkboard sign announced BOOK NOOK in perky, brightly colored letters.

In the coffee shop part, a few people were working on laptops, and a kid—probably about nine or ten—sat at a corner table, turning pages in a giant book Annabelle recognized. One of the fantasy novels Jeremy had been into a couple of summers ago.

There was a woman behind the counter with lightly freckled skin and hair that color of red that was almost definitely dyed—all one shade and red-red, not the orangey-brown or orangey-blond people *called* red. She was steaming milk in a little silver pitcher.

The milk hissing stopped, and then the redhead adjusted the green bandana that was attempting to hold back her hair. "Darn. I made your mocha full-caf instead of half-caf, Jenny," she announced. "Anybody want a free drink?"

The boy reading the giant book perked up, and she gave him a quick head shake.

"Anybody old enough to have coffee want a free drink?"

One of the guys behind a laptop held up his hand to claim it.

Maybe Dad wasn't working today. Relief washed over Annabelle, as if she didn't want to see him after all.

But that had to be leftover from what things had been like before. She *did* want to see him now. That's why she'd come all this way!

Her stomach growled loud enough that the free drink claimer looked at her.

"What can I do for you, hon?" the redheaded lady asked.

Annabelle scanned the price cards nestled among the pastries. A dollar and eighty cents wasn't enough to buy anything. Maybe she had more change?

She took out her wallet and balanced it in her bad hand as she rummaged for nickels and dimes with her good one.

And then he came out of the back room, humming along to the music. Her dad.

She set down her wallet on a nearby table, not even bothering to close it.

His hair, almost the same shade as hers, was cut shorter than she'd ever seen it, and she'd never seen his face so tan. She would have assumed his skin didn't really get tan, like hers didn't. And she didn't ever remember him *humming.* He locked eyes with the redhead, and there was something about the way they looked at each other—as if they were having a whole conversation with their eyes. Annabelle was positive: She was the "friend" he'd moved with. And she wasn't just a friend.

He was balancing a tray of pastries on one arm, and he went out of his way to pass by the kid's table and ruffle his hair the way Mitch ruffled Annabelle's.

Her heart ached, suddenly, for Mitch's hair-ruffling and blown kisses and strategizing sessions. And for Mom's clinking bracelets and jasmine perfume and extra-tight hugs. Even for her annoying habit of getting everything monogrammed.

She didn't know this man who was humming and winking and carrying pastries. Not really—not anymore.

He hadn't spotted her yet. She could leave.

"Did you decide, hon?" the redhead asked.

Then there was a clang as Dad set the tray of pastries on top of the glass display case. The tray tipped forward, and the redhead reached out to steady it. A cinnamon roll fell to the ground.

"Annie," Dad said.

Annabelle didn't like it, the way the old nickname sounded out loud.

"Annie" was a little girl who lived in New Jersey and

barely knew Mitch and had no idea she needed tutoring and learning plans and accommodations. Or that she'd break all the pool's under-fourteen butterfly records, either.

"What—what are you doing here?" he sputtered.

"You're Annabelle," the woman said. "My God."

"Who's Annabelle?" asked the kid with the book.

The redhead gave Dad a little shove, and he finally came around to where Annabelle was standing. As he hugged her, she had a flash of being a little kid just barely able to grab onto his middle. Now her chin fit over his shoulder and his stubble scratched her cheek.

"Look at you," he said. "Wow."

Annabelle had never understood that expression. It sounded like an instruction, but she *couldn't* look at herself right at that moment, even if she wanted to. Instead, she looked over Dad's shoulder at the menu written on a chalkboard on the wall.

There were two salads, a bunch of drinks, and a few sandwiches.

GREG'S GRILLED CHEESE! was written in the same cheerful handwriting from the Book Nook sign. NEW! PEACH, BRIE, AND BACON.

Not the kind with strawberries and goat cheese. The sandwich he'd made for Annabelle wasn't even on there anymore. And she hated brie. The crusty white stuff on the outside grossed her out.

"Who's Annabelle?" the kid with the giant book asked again.

This kid—the redhead's son, he had to be—Dad had never told him about his daughter?

Dad didn't answer. His eyes darted from the kid to Annabelle and back.

His letter had said he missed her every day. His email had said he was thrilled to hear from her. That he wanted her to visit—that she was welcome any time!

But now that she'd come, he just stood there. He wore a navy T-shirt with gray trim that she actually recognized, but it was frayed around the collar. Last time Annabelle had seen it, it had still been new.

He cleared his throat. "Can I get you something? A . . . hot chocolate? Or a cookie? On the house."

"I'll take a cookie!" the kid piped up.

"Finn," the redhead warned, but Annabelle's dad smiled at the kid. And as he did, his face relaxed.

This boy read enormous books for fun and could make her father smile for real. A *comfortable* smile. A smile that said this was all part of a routine, this kid asking for a treat he wasn't going to get, even though he knew he wasn't going to get it.

And this boy didn't even know Annabelle existed. Annabelle usually corrected people when they thought

Mitch was her dad. But her dad hadn't even told this kid her name.

How much could he really have missed her, then? How important to him could she actually be?

"I'm sorry," Annabelle said. "I can't stay."

"But you came all this way," the redhead said.

Not Dad. *Dad* didn't tell her to stay. Dad didn't say anything.

It wasn't the same as that time when he'd shown up drunk at swim practice and then left without apologizing. But in a way, it wasn't all that different. He wasn't stepping up and *doing* anything. He was just looking at her as if he didn't know how to handle the fact that she was there. As if it would maybe be easier for him if she *wasn't*.

And here she'd let herself believe he moved to Boston to be close to her. How clueless could she be?

"I—I didn't think you'd come so soon," her dad said. "Without any notice."

He rubbed his hand over the back of his neck. She'd forgotten that he did that.

So he hadn't meant it when he said she could visit anytime. He had his own life now, and he needed "notice" to make room for her.

"I'm here for a concert," she lied. "With my friends.

I just happened to be right nearby. I should get back to them."

She didn't wait for a response. She turned to bolt and nearly collided with two girls who were approaching the counter. Her bag slipped down her good arm as she ducked out of their path. The salt-and-pepper granite rock skittered across the tiled floor, landing under a table where nobody was sitting. And even though it was only a silly rock and there were tons more like it on every single beach on Gray Island, she didn't want to leave it here, so she got down on her knees to pick it up. She forgot that she couldn't push off of her right hand as she stood back up, and pain shot up her arm as she dashed toward the door.

"Annabelle, wait!" a voice called.

But it was only the redhead again, so she kept on going, out the door with those cheerful bells that jangled when it opened.

"You don't have to go!" the redhead said, rushing out to follow.

Dad followed, too . . . sort of. But he stood a few steps behind the redhead, all wide-eyed and hesitant, holding the door open but not actually coming outside.

He looked a whole lot like Jeremy had last summer when he and Annabelle and Mia had stood in line for the biggest roller coaster at an amusement park, and then he'd decided he didn't actually want to go on when they finally got to the front.

But Jeremy was a *kid*, and Dad was supposed to be an *adult*. Dad was supposed to welcome her and know what to say and what to do, not stand there all freaked out.

"I really do have to meet my friends," Annabelle insisted.

Dad cleared his throat. "We'll . . . see you soon, I hope," he said.

Right. It was obvious he didn't *really* hope that.

Annabelle took off toward the T stop, and when she turned around to check one last time, the door to the coffee shop was closed and the redhead had gone back inside. The sidewalk was completely empty, with the bright afternoon sun perched high in the sky, as if nothing had happened at all.

Chapter 30

The T came right away, so at least Annabelle didn't have to wait there in her dad's neighborhood. If she hurried, she could make the next bus to the Cape. There wasn't any real reason to rush back when all that waited for her on Gray Island was her worried, probably furious mom and a whole bunch of people who were glad they weren't as pathetic as she was, but still. She wanted to be back at her house or at the little beach down the road, where she could walk up and down the shore, picking up shells and rocks and listening to the familiar swish of the ocean—in and out, high tide and low tide. A little rougher some days and calmer other days, but always vast and moving and *there*.

What had she been thinking, showing up to see her dad out of nowhere as if she could fit herself into his new life like the last piece in a puzzle?

When the train pulled into the station, Annabelle pushed through the crowds, apologizing as she cut off a hobbling older lady. Once she got to the bus terminal, she hurried to line up in the right place.

Then she dug into her purse to get her wallet, where she'd left her bus and ferry tickets to keep them safe. Her hand hit her phone, the rock, her house keys, a pack of gum, and a ChapStick.

No wallet.

Her CharlieCard had been in the pocket of her shorts, but her wallet was gone.

Over the loudspeaker, a voice with a strong Boston accent announced that the bus to Hyannis was boarding. Annabelle's throat went dry.

She'd had her wallet out at the coffee shop when she was counting her change. She could see it now, sitting open on that table, a few coins in the change purse and her Gray Island Academy ID card peeking through the clear slot. She hadn't picked it up before she left.

"Miss? You in line or not?" asked a man behind her.

"I can't—I don't—" Annabelle stammered.

"Sweetheart, you're right in the way," a woman said. "If you're not going to Hyannis, you need to get out of the line."

She backed away, crashing into the line divider and knocking the pole to the ground, where it landed with a clang that made her jump.

"Geez, watch it!" someone said.

She tried to pick it up with her good hand, but it was heavier than she'd realized. It fell back over and clanged against the ground again.

She was light-headed with hunger and all of these people were watching her as she walked over to an empty bench after she'd made this huge scene, but somehow she felt oddly calm.

Here she was, stuck at a giant bus station in Boston, with no way to get anything to eat and no way to get home. Right when she thought she couldn't possibly have screwed everything up any worse.

She pulled out her phone. Jeremy was close by for his summer program, but it wasn't like he would want to see her, and what could he do?

She could call Mom, but it would be hours before Mom could get all the way here, and Mom was going to be so, so upset. Mitch would know what to do, probably. He'd come up with a strategy. He was her best option.

Unless . . . Connor and his friends were coming for the concert, and when Mark had rattled off the names of people who were coming, he hadn't said Caroline's. Maybe they had an extra ticket still, even?

But no. Connor was with Caroline, and that whole fantasy about seeing him here at the station was just a ridiculous, delusional dream.

Annabelle took a deep breath and powered on her phone. She knew message after message would pop up from Mom, but she wasn't going to read them. She was going to call Mitch and ask him what to do, and that was all.

Except then she *couldn't* ignore all of the messages that flashed across the screen, because she saw Connor's name.

How's it going, HB? he'd written.

Three and a half hours ago. *Today.*

After the other night with Caroline, he still wanted to talk to her. And he was probably on his way to this very station where she was sitting right now.

She clicked on his number and dialed.

Connor picked up on the third ring. "Hello?"

People were talking in the background, but Annabelle couldn't make out what they were saying. Connor's voice sounded soft but close, as if he were talking right into the phone with his hand covering his mouth.

"Um, are you in Boston?" she asked.

There was a pause, and Jordan's seagull laugh blared in the background.

"Why?" Connor asked.

It wasn't an easy question to answer. "Well, I . . . I am, and I sort of need . . . I'm stuck."

"You're stuck?" Connor asked.

It wasn't mean, the way he said it. It was just kind of *thin*. Off-handed and a little confused. Like it wasn't really his problem if she was in trouble.

Just like it hadn't really been his problem when she was in trouble the night they tried to get into Dennis Martin's pool, she realized.

"Con, who're you talking to?" a girl's voice asked.

Annabelle struggled to swallow. "Is that Caroline?"

Another long pause. "Yeah. Look, I'm on the bus, and I don't really . . ." He trailed off.

Tears blurred Annabelle's eyes, but she willed them to stay out of her voice. "I saw your text."

No response.

"Why did you text me?" she asked.

She didn't only mean this afternoon. She wanted to know why he'd kept on texting her all those other times, too. And why he'd flicked her ponytail, and why he'd stared at her the way he'd stared at her when all that time he'd had *Caroline*.

"I was just making sure we were good," Connor said. "That you were good. That you weren't . . ."

He didn't bother to finish that sentence, either. Or maybe he couldn't, with Caroline right there.

Annabelle had never been good at the fill-in questions on Mr. Derrickson's history tests, but she was pretty sure she knew how to fill in the rest of Connor's sentence. He wanted to be sure that she wasn't mad at him. That she still thought he was so great and wonderful, like Elisa had said.

A voice came on the intercom again. The Hyannis bus was leaving with all those other people but not her.

"Right," she said. "Bye, Connor."

She hung up without waiting for him to say anything else and buried her head in her hands.

What was *wrong* with her? She couldn't believe she'd called Connor as if she really thought he'd rush over to rescue her just because he sent *one* meaningless text that took basically *zero* effort.

That was even more pathetic than showing up at that party when she hadn't been invited and sitting down next to him in the sand. Even more pathetic than assuming she'd fit with her dad when she hadn't seen him in ages and the bad memories were so much stronger than the good ones, like flashlights shining steady instead of fireflies blinking their faint glow.

Her phone buzzed with a new text from Connor. **Sorry HB.** ☹

She stared at those two flimsy words—one he hadn't even typed out all the way—and that lazy, empty frowny face. A sharp new feeling knocked a little bit of her shame out of the way and made her sit up straighter.

Anger.

She was angry with herself, yes.

But she was angry with Connor, too.

Sorry, he'd texted.

Well, *she* was sorry, too. She was sorry for the version of herself who'd heard Connor say she was all grown up when she stepped out of the pool that day and gotten so excited about what that might mean.

And she was sorry for rosy-cheeked Caroline, all snuggled up next to Connor on the bus right now, with no idea how he treated other girls.

She thought of Connor running over to congratulate her after her second meet with the team. Rushing so he wouldn't miss her, with his goggles pushed up against his forehead and those red goggle indents ringing his bright green eyes.

She imagined herself grabbing the front of those goggles, pulling as hard as she could, and letting them go—*snap!*—so they'd smash right into his handsome, flirtatious, confident, charming face.

Then she closed his last text message and called the person she should have called in the first place.

"Belle!" Mom said before the phone even finished ringing once. "Stay right where you are, baby. I'll be there in ten minutes."

Mom had come straight to Boston as soon as she'd gotten the text Annabelle had sent this morning.

She'd taken the car on the ferry, and she'd been on her way to the college where Jeremy's summer program was, figuring Annabelle might have gone there. Then Dad had called her after Annabelle had left the coffee shop, so she'd started heading in that direction instead. And when Annabelle had finally turned her cell phone back on, Mom had tracked it to the station and was already on her way there.

Mom ran up to where Annabelle was waiting, in front of the soft pretzel place, and pulled her in for a long, tight hug.

"I'm so sorry," Annabelle said. "I'm sorry I always make you worried and I keep messing everything up."

Mom pulled away, and the line between her eyebrows looked different this close up. Concerned instead of worried. Those two words sounded pretty close to the same thing, but they weren't.

Concerned was the opposite of how Connor's voice had sounded when she told him she was stuck.

"Honey, you don't always make me worried," Mom said. "Why would you think that?"

"Because . . . school, and then . . . Connor, and my hand."

Mom held on to Annabelle's good hand and led her back over to the empty bench where she'd been sitting before.

"Annabelle. You make me happy and proud. And sure, sometimes a little worried. But I don't know any moms who don't worry about their kids. It goes with the territory."

"But . . . Saturday night, you and Mitch sounded so happy before you knew I was home. When it was just the two of you. I'm not like you. I mess everything up."

Mom was still holding Annabelle's hand, and now she squeezed it tight. "Do you know what Mitch and I did after you went to bed Saturday night? We watched all the videos he had on his phone of you racing this summer. Swimming so much faster than those girls who were twice your size. Getting right back up there after you got disqualified."

Annabelle had been staring down at the three thin bracelets on Mom's arm, but now she picked up her head. "Why?"

"Because you amaze us, Belle. How hard you work? The way you don't give up even when something goes wrong?" Mom angled her head down a little, making sure Annabelle was looking right into her eyes. "That's brave, honey. That's strong."

Usually, Mom's compliments didn't fill Annabelle up the way Mitch's did. When Mom told her she did great in a swim meet, she didn't really know what she was talking about. And when she said she was proud of Annabelle for working hard at school, it felt like she'd be prouder if Annabelle's grades were as good as Jeremy's or Mia's. But this time, the compliment warmed up Annabelle's whole body. Not that hot-chocolate warmth in her belly, like she'd gotten with Connor, but a gentler, more even warmth, like stepping out into the sun.

"I mean, I'd rather you didn't hop on a ferry by yourself to track down your father," Mom said. "But I'm not worried about you in the grand scheme of things. I worry day-to-day, sure. But I know you're going to be okay. You hear me?"

Annabelle nodded, and her stomach growled. "I haven't eaten since breakfast."

Mom stood and surveyed the area. "Then how does a greasy, sugary pretzel sound?"

"Really, really good," Annabelle said, and they walked up to the pretzel counter, hand in hand.

Chapter 31

On the drive to Cape Cod, Mom told Annabelle that Dad had called her in the spring, back when he'd first moved to Boston.

"He said he wanted to be in touch with you," she said. "I should have told you right away."

Mom was watching the road, and Annabelle studied her profile. She and Mom had different coloring—Mom's hair and eyes were darker—but Mitch always said how much they looked alike from the side because they had the same chin and nose.

All this time, Annabelle had thought she was keeping something from her mom, but her mom had been keeping it from her, too?

"Why didn't you tell me?" she asked.

Mom sighed. "It wasn't the first time I had heard from him. He used to leave messages sometimes, saying how much he missed you. How he wanted to talk to you or visit, but then . . . he didn't follow through."

Mom paused and mushed her lips together. It looked a lot like she might be biting her bottom lip the way she always told Annabelle not to.

"I didn't want you to be disappointed if you didn't hear from him. I thought . . ." She paused again, and now she was *definitely* biting her lip. "I misunderstood. I told him he could write to you when he was ready, but I thought he'd tell me before he sent a letter. I thought I'd be able to prepare you. To talk through what it would feel like to hear from him."

Annabelle remembered pulling that square envelope out of the stack of mail and seeing his handwriting. She wasn't sure anything would have prepared her for that, really, whether Mom had told her the letter was coming or not.

Traffic slowed down on the highway, and Mom glanced over. "I'm sorry, honey," she said. Which was bizarre. *Annabelle* had kept the letter a secret and snuck away to Boston, and Mom was apologizing. "I wanted to protect you, and I couldn't."

She thought of Kayla and Elisa. How they'd been trying to protect her, too, but that hadn't worked, either. How maybe she had to make her own mistakes with Dad and with Connor, as humiliating as they were.

"I'm sorry, too," she told Mom.

"I know, honey." Mom patted Annabelle's hand, and her bracelets clinked. "We'll have to talk about some consequences for what happened today, but it's okay. It's all going to be okay."

And Annabelle felt like maybe that was true. Especially after they got back to the ferry terminal in Cape Cod, and Mom told Annabelle something else she'd never known: the real reason Mitch had wanted to move to the island two years ago.

"It's true that the house was a good deal. And it *was* brave and entrepreneurial. But some investments he'd made hadn't done so well. We *needed* to sell the New Jersey house; we didn't choose to."

At first, Annabelle thought she must have misheard. *Mitch*, the "mover and shaker" who got profiled in *Gray Island Magazine*, had made bad investments?

"Maybe I've pushed too hard for you to be at the Academy," Mom added as they parked the car on the bottom level of the ferry. "I felt guilty that the public schools were so highly ranked in New Jersey, and here we were pulling you out of them because moving to the island was right for *us*, not for *you*. But maybe the Academy just isn't a good fit."

Annabelle tested out the idea of leaving the Academy, the way she sometimes pressed against the slowly healing bone in her thumb to see how much it still hurt. It didn't feel good . . . but it wasn't *quite* so sharply painful anymore.

"When we met with Mrs. Sloane," Mom went on. "I don't know. I don't want you to be at a school where they don't appreciate you."

Wait. Where *they* didn't appreciate *her*?

Mom had always been a teacher-is-always-right parent, never listening to excuses about how some teacher was mean or unfair or didn't assign something until the last minute. Annabelle had assumed that if she left the Academy, it would be because she wasn't right for the school, not the other way around.

They climbed the stairs to the ferry's top deck, where they could watch their progress across the open ocean and then see the familiar black-and-white Bruck Point Lighthouse as the island came into view.

"Well, we don't have to decide anything today," Mom said.

So they didn't. They bought Hershey bars at the snack stand and didn't care when the chocolate melted all over their hands. And Mom helped Annabelle find some more Dad memories—good ones, like how he'd taken her to her first swimming lessons when she was two, and how he used to push her on the swing at the park down the road for hours and make up silly songs to help her remember her spelling words.

"He really does love you," Mom said. "So much, honey. I hope he'll be able to show you that someday."

And when they got back home and Mitch hugged Annabelle, she knew deep in her gut that she could quit swimming forever, and she and Mitch would find new things to bond over. He would ruffle her hair and blow her kisses, anyway.

"It can be tough stuff, being a dad," he said. "I know yours disappointed you today, but I want you to know: I've done my share of disappointing things, too."

She didn't know what he meant at first.

But then she remembered his daughter Maura at the pool last summer, when he was criticizing the parents who let their kids wear swimmies. How she said he wasn't around to watch her learn to swim when she was a kid. And she thought of that boy at the coffee shop, Finn. How Finn was getting a different version of her dad than she had. One that hummed and grinned and got tan in the summer.

It wasn't really fair, the idea that she was getting a version of Mitch that his own daughters hadn't. But he was trying to make things right with them. He called them every Sunday and agonized over how to make things special whenever they visited.

"Well, you've never disappointed me," she said.

"Right back atcha, kiddo," he replied. *"Never."*

Chapter 32

Later that week, Annabelle made a plan to meet Elisa and Kayla at Beach Buzz after one of Elisa's shifts.

It was a rainy day, so the coffee shop was extra busy, but they pulled an extra chair over to a two-person table by the window.

All three of them were quiet when they first sat down, and then all three of them started speaking at the same time.

"So, listen," Elisa started at the same time as Kayla said, "We didn't mean to upset you," and Annabelle said, "I'm really sorry about the other night."

"Jinx!" Elisa called out, and they all laughed.

Then they were quiet again, not wanting to cut each other off. Annabelle thought of the orientation she, Jeremy, and Mia had gone to at the Academy before sixth grade, with all the other day students. They did this activity where they had to count to ten as a group, but they couldn't plan out what order they would go in, and they had to start over any time two people said a number at the same time.

They'd messed up again and again until Mia had taken over, counting to ten as fast as she could all by herself. When the admissions person had pointed out that the idea was to work together, Mia had said, "We did! I said the numbers and everybody else didn't interrupt me."

Annabelle channeled some of sixth-grade Mia's confidence and blurted out what she wanted to say.

"You were right about Connor. About how he was acting with me. It didn't mean anything. I should have listened to you, and I shouldn't have just left."

Kayla spun around the straw in her drink. "Well, we probably shouldn't have, like, bombarded you."

Elisa nodded. "As soon as you left, we realized you probably felt kind of cornered."

"A little," Annabelle admitted. "But I get it now. You were trying to look out for me."

"Sorry if we kind of bungled it, though," Elisa said.

"And we're really sorry if Connor hurt you," Kayla added.

Annabelle had thought the Connor-hurt had already crested, but it hit her again at full force. "I should have realized," she squeaked. "I shouldn't have been so—"

"Hang on," Elisa stopped her. "You can't beat yourself up about this, Annabelle. It's impossible not to be into it when someone like Connor is giving you that kind of attention."

The way she said it, Annabelle got the impression she was speaking from experience.

"Did you . . ." She wasn't sure how to finish the question she wanted to ask, but Elisa seemed to understand.

"We had a thing last summer. Or, I thought it was a thing." Elisa's voice was casual, but she tore off pieces of her napkin as she spoke. One corner, then the next, then the next. "We were close, and it seemed like it meant something, but then I found out it didn't."

She didn't explain how she found that out, and Annabelle's throat went dry as she remembered the way Connor had laughed at the pool when Jordan had called Elisa manly. Her heart hurt for last-summer Elisa almost as much as it hurt for herself.

"Well, now you have somebody way better to flirt with," Kayla whispered to Elisa, glancing over toward the counter. Elisa's eyes darted over, too, and Annabelle followed her gaze.

The guy who was working was tall with brown skin and short hair. When he noticed Elisa looking, he motioned for her to come over.

"Hey!" he said, pointing at the specials board. "What's with this new drink? Chai-infused oatmilk?"

Elisa's freckled cheeks flamed pink.

"Go," Kayla urged. "Teach him how to make the oaty-chai magic!"

Elisa tossed her ripped-up napkin at Kayla, but she was beaming as she walked to the counter.

Kayla had gotten a giant muffin, and she pushed the plate toward Annabelle. "You want any? It's blackberry thyme. The thyme's kind of weird, but not bad as long as you know it's coming."

Annabelle took a little piece and watched Kayla tear one off, too.

She bit her bottom lip instead of eating the piece of muffin. Kayla had tried to talk to her about Connor even though that was obviously uncomfortable, but Annabelle had never said anything about where Kayla had been last summer and what she was recovering from. She still wasn't sure how to talk about it, but she should at least try.

"Um, I know I've never really said anything about . . . when you were sick. And how you were at the treatment place last summer. I'm sorry you had to go through that. It must have been really hard. And I'm really happy you're better."

Kayla pushed her bangs out of her eyes, and the gesture made her look even more like Jeremy than usual.

"It's still pretty hard," she said. "But thanks. For saying that."

"You're welcome." Annabelle took a sip of her lemonade, which was the perfect balance of tart and sweet. She was glad she hadn't tried to order some kind of coffee drink just because the older girls did. "How's Jeremy?"

Kayla took a bite of muffin. "He's good, I think. Though I'm sure he'd be better if you guys made up."

Annabelle's cheeks burned, so she took another sip to cool them down. "I want to fix things when he gets back."

"Good," Kayla said, nodding as if that had fixed the situation already, just knowing that Annabelle wanted to make things right.

Annabelle pictured Jeremy's hurt, angry face and was pretty sure it wasn't going to be that easy. But she was also pretty sure she would figure something out.

After Annabelle said goodbye to Kayla and Elisa, she put on her raincoat and walked up the street to meet Mitch at his office for lunch.

But on her way, she peeked into the window of the bagel place, and there was Mia, by herself at one of the front tables. She almost kept going, but then she changed her mind and went in.

"Hey." She slid off the hood of her coat and approached Mia's table.

Mia's dark eyes went wide with surprise. "Oh. Hey."

She was wearing the bright pink shirt she'd gotten on that shopping trip in the spring. Annabelle had bought the same one in light blue, and Mia had chosen a pale green one at first, but her mom had vetoed that, saying pale colors did nothing for Mia's complexion and she had to "go bold" if she wanted to stand out.

"What are you up to?" Annabelle asked, and Mia held up what was left of her bagel as if to say, *What does it look like?*

Right. Annabelle was about ready to give up and leave, but then Mia heaved an enormous sigh.

"I have literally nothing to do until practice, and practice is probably going to get canceled if there's lightning. Reagan went back to Connecticut and Jeremy's in Boston and Genevieve's babysitting and I don't know what any of the other swim team girls are doing. So I'm stuck here on this tiny, boring island eating this bagel as slowly as I can to kill time."

Annabelle stared at Mia, remembering what rainy days had been like last summer.

Once, the two of them had made scavenger hunts for each other inside Mia's house. Another time they'd found five different cookie recipes—peanut butter, chocolate chip, double chocolate, oatmeal raisin, and snickerdoodles—and combined the best parts of each recipe into a batch of mash-up cookies, even though Mia's mom told them there was no way all those things would taste good together. The cookies *were* pretty terrible, but Mia had insisted she loved them, and Annabelle had choked down a couple in solidarity.

Annabelle didn't think Mia had ever been bored last summer. She hadn't waited around for other people to invite her along to plans. She'd *made* the plans.

Annabelle wished she could say, *I'll hang out with you today. You name the plan and I'll do it!*

But she couldn't forget that Mia had seemed sort of happy when she'd messed things up with Connor. She was tired of feeling like Mia was keeping a tally of all the assignments she did badly on at school. And she didn't want to be the kind of person she'd become around Mia this summer, either. The kind of person who left Mia out on purpose and wanted her to be jealous.

Maybe all the competitiveness between them had ruined their friendship completely, or maybe there still *could* be something good between them if they gave themselves a little break. She really wasn't sure.

She thought of that blackberry-thyme muffin—how Kayla had said the thyme wasn't bad as long as you knew it was coming. How lots of things would be easier if you knew what was coming, but that's almost never how things went.

It was a tiny island, though, like Mia had said. They weren't going to lose track of each other. If there was some part of their friendship left to salvage once the bad feelings had passed, they had time.

"This summer hasn't gone the way I wanted it to at all," Annabelle said.

She braced herself for Mia to say something X-Acto-knife sharp again, about how Annabelle shouldn't have ditched her and Jeremy or thrown herself at Connor.

But Mia said, "Me neither. I kind of . . . I miss last summer."

"Me too," Annabelle agreed.

But she wouldn't choose to go back to last summer if someone offered her the option.

She didn't want to have to live through the most

humiliating moments of this summer again—that was part of it. But she wouldn't want them wiped away, either.

She thought of that first-day-of-summer-break Annabelle again, so discouraged after her history exam and so excited when Connor noticed her. She was glad for all the ways she'd changed since that day, even though she wasn't glad about all the things that had changed her.

"Well, I'm meeting Mitch, so I should probably go," she finally said.

Mia nodded. "Okay. Cheerio, Annabelle," she said, using their silly old goodbye.

"Ta-ta, Mia," Annabelle replied.

And she went out into the rain, breathing in the sweet, fresh smell of it and not really minding the way it drenched her bare legs and made her flip-flops all squeaky and slippery.

Chapter 33

Back home that afternoon, Annabelle took apart her old shell lamp and then scattered the perfect, store-bought shells along the rain-drop-speckled sand at the little beach. She decided it wasn't so helpful to have something that looked so pretty but wasn't real. Like that necklace Mrs. Sloane wore, with the pink quartz pendant that was too shiny and round.

For now, the only things she kept in the bottom of the lamp were the broken shell from Kelsey Bennett and the salt-and-pepper granite stone from that awful night with Connor.

At first, looking at the stone had made her cringe with shame. But it was strong, that rock. Strong enough to survive getting tossed around by waves and buried under sand. And Annabelle wanted to be strong, too.

Even if that meant doing scary, embarrassing things, like sitting on the bad-kid bench outside of Mrs. Sloane's office while everyone else was in foreign language class, because maybe dropping Spanish really *would* help her do better in eighth grade. And apologizing to Jeremy.

The day after Jeremy got home from his summer program, Annabelle got a ride to his house. She was waiting on his front steps when Mrs. Green's car pulled into the driveway after swim practice.

"Annabelle!" Mrs. Green said. "What a nice surprise." Then she mouthed, "Good luck," and headed inside.

It had been a month since Annabelle had seen Jeremy, and his hair had grown enough that the front part reached his eyebrows again. He didn't get out of the car right away, even though she knew he'd seen her.

She walked over to the car holding up the slightly melted to-go cup of ice cream she'd picked up at the Creamery and brought over in a cooler. A large, with half double chocolate chunk and half peanut butter cup. And eventually, he opened the car door.

"I brought a peace offering," she said. "And I won't laugh at you if you end up with chocolate lipstick, I promise."

Jeremy didn't smile, but he took the ice cream and

followed her over to the front steps. She sat on the bottom one, and he took the top.

"I'm sorry I was awful to you," she said. "And thank you for helping me that night when I got hurt. I was wrong to go along with everyone, and I was really wrong to get mad at you when . . ." This part still wasn't easy to say, even though she knew it was true. "When you were right. About Connor not really caring and everything. And you were just being a good friend."

Jeremy nodded as he pried the top off the ice cream and took his first bite. "It's okay," he said finally.

"It's kind of not, though," Annabelle said. "I'm sorry I was such an idiot."

Jeremy's head snapped up just like Mom's did if she ever heard Annabelle use that word. "Don't say that. You're not an idiot."

"Yeah, right," she said, forcing out a fake little laugh.

"You're not," Jeremy said. His voice was louder this time.

"Well, I was stupid to get all caught up in Connor and being on the high school team and . . ." She made herself say it. "I'm not smart like you and Mia."

Jeremy pushed his chocolate scoop to the side a bit and handed the cup to Annabelle. "Duh," he said, and it stung, even though it was true. But then he added, "You're smart like *you*."

Her cheeks heated up even as she brought a cold spoonful of ice cream to her mouth.

That wasn't true, was it?

She remembered how smart she'd felt last summer at the shark museum, when Mr. Green took her and Jeremy and the people there assumed she knew as much as he did. And back in sixth-grade science, when Mrs. Mattson always told her how perceptive she was.

Maybe it *was* perceptive of her to know exactly when another swimmer was getting tired so she could pick up her pace and to notice the ways Mia was changing to fit with her new friends.

"I'm glad you're home," she told Jeremy. And his smile—that sweet smile that told everybody what a nice guy he was before he even opened his mouth to speak— spread across his face right away.

"Me too."

They sat there for a while, eating their ice cream and waving away bugs that flew too close. When they finished, Jeremy sipped up the milky, sweet liquid that was left at the bottom of the cup, just like he always did, and when he tipped his head forward again, his whole chin was covered with chocolate.

"You look like a little kid," Annabelle told him as she handed him a stack of napkins.

"Who cares?" he said.

And who *did* care, really? There were worse things than being like a little kid sometimes.

He wiped off his chin and then lunged toward her face with the chocolaty napkin he'd used, as if he were going to smear it on her cheek. She laughed and pushed his hand away.

"You wanna go see the seals on Saturday?" he asked. "The app says Bertha's coming north again. Maybe we'll spot her at Bluff Point going after a seal."

Annabelle tried to grab a napkin back to wipe a dribble of ice cream off her arm, but when Jeremy held the napkins behind his back, she gave up and licked it off.

"Definitely," she said. "But you don't really want to see a great white shark, do you?"

Last summer when they'd gone out on Mia's family's boat, a dolphin had come pretty close to the bow, and Jeremy had been so surprised he'd screamed. Mia had teased him about it the whole rest of the day.

"I guess not," he said. "But it would be pretty amazing to see one and not panic, wouldn't it? To be brave enough to just appreciate how amazing it is, you know?"

Annabelle nodded. She didn't have any desire to see Bertha for real, but she was pretty sure she understood why Jeremy felt that way.

If he were brave enough to see a white shark without freaking out, he might feel like *he* fit better with his fearless dad. Annabelle had seen the way Mr. Green's face had lit up with pride when he watched Jeremy win third place at the big mathlete tournament on the Cape last winter, though. She was pretty sure his dad cared more about all the things Jeremy did well than whether or not he would be scared to spot a shark or whether or not he won any swim team races.

"Wait, I thought you said Bertha's not old enough to eat a seal," Annabelle said.

Jeremy stood up and held a hand out to her. "Doesn't mean she can't try," he said, and Annabelle held out hers—nearly healed now—and let him gently pull her up to standing.

Chapter 34

The next morning, Annabelle and Mitch got up early and went down to the little beach before the sun got too strong. Annabelle didn't have to wear her brace anymore, and the physical therapist had cleared her to swim for real.

There wasn't a buoy out in the water to swim to, but Annabelle didn't need one. She knew how many strokes to take for every lap, and she didn't need a wall to push off of when she changed directions.

Mitch's two daughters were coming the next weekend, and Mitch was bubbling over with plans for all the things he wanted to do to make their visit special. And Mom and Mitch had encouraged Annabelle to email Dad when she was ready. They thought Dad had had the right idea—emailing back and forth to get to know each other a little bit again, and then maybe a phone call or two before they dove into seeing each other.

But for now, she was focusing on letting her wrist and thumb heal the rest of the way and getting ready for the school year in her tutoring sessions with Janine. And maybe even getting herself in good enough shape to be back for the last meet of the season—the rematch against South Shore—if Mom and Mitch agreed.

It would be pretty humiliating, showing up to see Connor and Jordan and Ruby and all of those people she'd embarrassed herself in front of.

But Kayla had come back to swim team this summer, even though everybody knew why she'd missed last season and nobody knew what to say about it. And Elisa had been hurt by Connor, too, but she hadn't let that get in her way. And Annabelle had already survived plenty of other humiliating things and kept on going.

She might not be fast enough to help the team win the medley relay and beat South Shore out for the league championship after not swimming for a month. And she might not be able to do any better in Mr. Derrickson's history class next year, either. But that didn't mean she couldn't try.

"I think I'm ready to keep up today," Mitch said as they walked down the beach a little bit, away from the sandbar, and waded in until the water was deep enough to start.

"Good luck with that," Annabelle told him.

Then she pulled down her goggles, kicked her feet off against the sand, and began to swim. The cold, salty water prickled her skin, and the gentle current of the tiny waves gave her just enough resistance to make her feel powerful enough to do almost anything as she pushed her body forward.

When she finally came up for air, she could hear the waves' steady rolling and Mitch's arms and legs splashing behind her, and then she was back underwater, blocking out everything but herself and propelling her body forward, out toward that infinite horizon.

Acknowledgments

I don't think I would have become a writer if I hadn't first become a middle school teacher, and I know I wouldn't have written this story if I hadn't been inspired by the students I taught and the conversations we had.

To all of my former students: Thank you for energizing me with your passion and creativity and for strengthening my resolve to write this kind of upper-middle-grade book. And very special thank yous to Lily Cappello and Madison Scheuer, who offered excellent advice about the swimming elements of this story, and to Dasha Sotnik-Platt, one of the most exuberant and prolific readers I've ever known, who read a book I'd written about Annabelle's stepsister and said, "I want Annabelle's story next." It took me several years, but here you go!

Sara Crowe, thank you for loving Annabelle back when she was a secondary character in Lissy's story and for urging me to keep writing this book. I so appreciate your enthusiasm and your hard work on my behalf.

Maggie Lehrman, thank you for believing that we need stories like Annabelle's and for guiding me along to realize my vision for this book. You are calming, encouraging, and wise, and I'm especially glad you helped me develop the girl power at the core of this story. Thank you to the awesome team at Abrams for contributing your many talents to creating this beautiful book. Nishant Choksi and Hana Anouk Nakamura, thank you for the incredible cover and book design. Jenny Choy, Trish McNamara O'Neill, Hallie Patterson, and Brooke Shearouse, thank you for all that you do to get my stories into the hands of readers.

Laura Sibson, thank you for helping me enrich the swimming scenes and understand Annabelle's unique intelligence . . . and for hosting me for many lovely writing dates and supplying me with delicious coffee and second breakfasts to keep me going. Jen Petro-Roy, thank you for your valuable insights about Kayla's character and eating disorder recovery. And Cordelia Jensen, my treasured friend and sometimes coauthor, thank you for reading this story more times than even my very specific memory can keep track of and for all the ways you helped me problem-solve and find the heart of this book. I am a better—and happier—writer because of you.

Writing can be a very solitary act and I am not a very

solitary person, so I feel lucky to be part of several writing communities. Thank you to the Vermont College of Fine Arts network, the Secret Gardeners (and especially our Philly contingent!), the Middle Grade at Heart crew, and the Electric Eighteens. The connections I have made with all of you have nourished my writing and brought me so much joy. Special shout-outs to my debut-year buddies Mary Winn Heider and Melissa Sarno and my publishing-expert buddies Lisa Leicht and Val Howlett; I'm so glad to have you as my friends and colleagues.

One of the best parts of becoming a published author has been the chance to engage with teachers and librarians who are passionate about connecting kids with books. I am so grateful to all the educators who have hosted me for school visits—especially my incredible former colleagues at Friends Select—and so inspired by all the educators I've met online and through nErDcamp events. I appreciate all that you do for your students and for authors!

Thank you, thank you, thank you to my friends, family members, and in-laws. You have been amazing about showing up to support my writing career—sometimes after flying long distances, sometimes with babies strapped to you, sometimes bearing shiny visors, and often buying multiple books to distribute—and I am endlessly grateful.

Thank you to my most generous supporter, my mom,

Elizabeth Morrison. Annabelle learns that she is smart, strong, and brave, and you have always made me feel that I am those things. You are the most loving mom, Grammy, and friend I can imagine.

Mike, thank you for being such a kind, patient, and fun partner and dad and for all the ways you show me how much you value my writing. Like Annabelle, I've had to learn to be careful not to talk myself into believing that other people are who I want them to be . . . but you are exactly who I hoped you would be and then some. And Cora and Sam, you amaze and delight me every day, and nothing brings me more joy than reading books with you. Thank you for being you.